The Fugitives

Helen May

 FriesenPress

Suite 300 - 990 Fort St
Victoria, BC, V8V 3K2
Canada

www.friesenpress.com

ISBN
978-1-5255-6643-1 (Hardcover)
978-1-5255-6644-8 (Paperback)
978-1-5255-6645-5 (eBook)

1. YOUNG ADULT FICTION, GIRLS & WOMEN

Distributed to the trade by The Ingram Book Company

Dedication:

My encouragement to all who practice grace of inclusion and protest vulgarity of exclusion.

Stay strong   Stay true.

Helen May

Contents

Prologue

Many centuries ago, the papacy in Rome, intent on converting rulers of countries in Europe and their people to Christianity, steadily extended its power beyond its borders. During that time, people who were considered to be infidels and heretics were hunted down, driven from their homes, their dwellings set on fire and often killed. The search focused on people who adhered to the Muslim faith and also on herbal healers and midwives. These women who assisted at births and ministered to the ill, as their grandmothers and great grandmothers had before them, were now forbidden to carry out their work and were marked as heretics. The church preached that salvation from sickness and childbirth — deemed to be God's punishment for living a sinful life — was the duty of the church to carry out. To enforce this law, a ruler and his church leaders recruited and trained young men to raid villages and rural communities in search of midwives and healers. Once captured, a woman was then tortured and publicly burned alive at the stake. Some were drowned.

Part One

Yunitra

Under smoke-filled skies a foul stench of death and destruction filled the air. Terrifying accounts of soldiers raiding villages in search of midwives and healers, whispered from one to another, spread through farming communities and village markets. These accounts described soldiers brandishing swords, setting dwellings on fire with flaming torches and killing anyone who resisted or attempted to flee. An aura of mourning took hold of inhabitants, fear stifled lively conversations between neighboring communities and destroyed all sense of hope.

To those who had been spared a raid, thus far, this merciless mayhem seemed to be an exaggeration but, to those whose loved ones had been wounded or killed and who had been forced to watch their homes burn, it was all too true.

Yunitra lived with her parents and aged grandmother in a village that had, as yet, been spared. Her parents, away all day working in a dry goods store that they owned, were content with the arrangement of Yunitra's care of her grandmother, Tallia, and also with her tending to the household chores. Tallia, although infirm and sensing that her life was coming to its end, determined that Yunitra learn as much as possible about the healing properties of plants. And so it was that most mornings after she had fed and bathed Tallia, Yunitra, guided by her grandmother, sketched plants, listing their uses while committing this information to memory. These quiet, gentle days in the company of Tallia, changed when Yunitra turned twelve and began work in her parents' store. She returned home for short periods throughout the day to see to Tallia's needs but that allowed no time for instruction on plants or sketching.

Initially, accounts of raids Yunitra overheard customers whispering about, had little effect on her until she realized that soldiers, although some distance away, as yet, were approaching their region. Suddenly she experienced a fear new to her and spoke to Tallia about this.

"Grandmother, why are soldiers searching for healers and midwives. . . please tell me and, oh, Grandmother, are we in danger?" "I've heard of this new law, my child – a law that forbids the worship of any deity that is not sanctioned by the church. Illness, infirmities – even giving birth – is deemed to be God's punishment. . . uh. . . for living sinfully. We are to believe that the power of the church leads to salvation from sin, and illness, that it is the duty of the church to do that - not healers and midwives. We could be in danger so we need to be silent and keep knowledge hidden."

Yunitra trusted the wisdom of her Grandmother but she could not accept that a ruler would order such actions to be carried out.

This cannot be right- to treat people this way – especially women who assist at births, heal the afflicted and provide comfort. Why does this ruler order the killing of those very women who ease the pain of others? And to destroy a community that is suspected to protect such a woman. . . Why? Perhaps Mama can also help me understand?

And so, Yunitra spoke out to her mother against what she believed to be this deep wrong and begged for an explanation.

"Yunitra! How dare you question the new law? You are drawing attention to our family and placing us all in danger! These mutinous words you so brazenly speak in this way will surely reach the church authorities. You should know better. I shall tell your father about this and ask him to silence you."

Yunitra soon discovered that her mother's words were not an idle threat.

From her bedroom window Yunitra observed her parents engaged in discussion at the far end of the garden. It was impossible to hear their words, but her mother was visibly agitated: her hands, extended towards Yunitra's father, sliced the air with angry jerks while the veins in her neck bulged and her mouth twisted as she spoke. Yunitra's father listened, his head lowered then suddenly a rigidity in his spine forced his head up to face his wife, his chin jutting forward, fisted hands at his side. With a curt nod he then turned and walked away. Yunitra's mother stood watching her husband's retreating back with a look that seemed to Yunitra, to be one of gloating triumph.

That curt nod her father had offered Yunitra's mother turned out be in agreement to seek audience with a church authority in a town far away. During the time that her father waited to be summoned Tallia died in her sleep. Now, Yunitra's grief over the loss of her close companion and mentor mixed with that fear she had felt over the news that soldiers were approaching the region and added to that her apprehension over the outcome of her father's visit with the church authority put her in an unaccustomed state of anxiety. As she struggled to resort to her natural optimism, she discovered a strength within that was to stand her in good stead in the coming months and years.

Yunitra's father upon his return from meeting with a church authority announced to his wife and daughter that he had begged the authorities to help them regain control of their daughter, to stem her dangerous questioning of the new law. And what was the outcome? Yunitra was sent away; away from her home, away from the village where she had lived all of her life of fourteen years. And if that were not enough of a punishment for asking questions, the authorities set penances to silence her: she would work at the Lodge for midwives and healers. She would serve the elderly and infirm. She would bathe fevered bodies; she would remove waste and fasten bandages; she would do as bidden without questions and in constant silence.

The night before Yunitra's departure she held a faint hope that her mother might have a change of mind or at least show some love and kindness but, instead, this is what she said to Yunitra: "You are an unruly, impetuous girl. Your unthinking behavior is putting your father and me in danger of losing our dry goods store and our home. And look at you - almost a woman and you still refuse to obey! This penance is all for your own good – a test of your faith to denounce your leaning towards heresy. One day you'll thank me."

Yunitra, lips drawn tightly closed, stood facing her mother, who handed to her two shapeless shifts –grey sack-like dresses – one of which her mother ordered she change into immediately. "To hide your body," she said while pulling at Yunitra's blouse and embroidered skirt as if these items of clothing had become emblematic of Yunitra's unseemly behavior.

The final item her mother insisted on was a head cloth of the same grey fabric to "bind that mess of unruly curls."

An acute feeling of betrayal knifing through Yunitra, silenced her. But her thoughts were not silenced. These were loud and thunderous:

But surely the Lodge in the forest is where midwives and healers do their work. . . if the frightening stories of midwives and healers are true then how can my parents. . . how could they even think, let alone carry out an order to put me to work alongside those who are in danger thereby endangering me, their daughter? A test, Mama said. . . I'm a heretic? But I learned well from Grandmother's mentoring. . . she wasn't wrong – was she?

Yunitra removed her blouse and skirt and dressed herself in the shapeless shift.

The Lodge

At sunrise the following morning Yunitra's father led her to the edge of the forest where the path to the Lodge began. Before turning away from her to return to the village he did not meet her eyes nor show any sign of regret. All he offered was a curt nod.

Yunitra, straight-backed and resolute, carrying a bundle that contained a tinderbox, a second shift and head cloth, set off down the path to the Lodge to the sound of her wooden clogs thudding with each step.

Well after mid-day Yunitra arrived at the Lodge, out of breath and thirsty. Her mind numb with apprehension, she knocked on a wide wooden door and waited. Not before too long, the door was opened partway by a tall slender grey-haired woman whose apron pockets bulged with rolled bandages. Taking a deep breath, Yuntra, hurried in case she lost her courage and burst out with her greeting: "With respect I greet you. My name is Yunitra. The authorities ordered that I work for you. They also ordered that I am to maintain complete silence. . . I am forbidden to speak from this moment on."

"You are welcome, my child. My name is Isabella. Please, come in."

Yunitra followed Isabella down the centre of a large room to a storage area at the back of the Lodge where bunches of herbs hanging to dry created a ceiling both fragrant and, somehow comforting. Isabella then handed to Yunitra a sleeping mat and a blanket indicating a corner to place her small bundle and also where she would sleep.

Yunitra soon familiarized herself with the daily routine of tasks she carried out and the simple layout of the Lodge's interior also became familiar and comfortable to work in. Built of hand-hewn logs and laid out in the shape of a T, there was ample space for at least 10 patients. The entrance - a wide wood door at the base of the 'T' opened directly into the area that accommodated patients. Poles supported a roof of interlaced saplings on top of which lay a solid roof of sod and moss. At the far end of the rectangular room where the T branched off to the left and to the right stood a massive hearth built of river stones where two cauldrons hung from iron hooks over a fire. Yunitra learned that one cauldron held soup and that she was to add to it, bones, herbs and vegetables every day. She was expected to be vigilant about the amount of water in the second cauldron as that was for bathing, laundry and for various medicinal infusions of herbal teas and poultices. The three midwives slept in the area to the right of the hearth. Herbs, tinctures and oils were prepared and stored in the area on the left which is where Yunitra's sleeping mat was laid out.

The midwives were kind and their words and instructions were simple as they gave her all the jobs that took no skill. They would not respond when she forgot her penance and asked a question and, that first night when she sang a lullaby, they said nothing.

It took a tremendous effort of will for Yunitra to maintain silence while her spirit struggled to assert itself. With so much to say, namely about her hurt and angry feelings over her parents' betrayal, she needed someone to talk to but she had been forbidden to speak. Her decision to concentrate on learning healing skills from the women in charge, helped control her emotions.

Each patient lay on a cloth-covered pallet of straw. Around each pallet, curtains suspended from the cross poles in the ceiling, provided privacy for the patient. Many were elderly suffering diseases of the lungs and also others with a palsy of the limbs that left them weak and frail. Recently though, an increasing number of people were coming to the Lodge with sword wounds that required attention and yet others with broken bones to be set. While Yunitra assisted, she listened to chilling accounts of cruelty and destruction carried out by raiding soldiers; accounts no different than those she had heard about when she was still at home. Her ire at the injustice and senseless cruelty rose as forcibly as it had before her penance. She steeled her resolve to keep learning, keep working and keep tending to the ill and wounded in her care.

Her days began before sunrise ministering to patients, replacing soiled bed linens with clean laundered ones, bathing one patient after another in water heated over the fire, rubbing their backs and chests with oils to relieve their breathing, propping them up into a sitting position in readiness for the meal of warm soup she had prepared. There were some whom she fed, others who had the strength to feed themselves.

The midwives and the patients grew to like this silent, hardworking girl whose smile seemed to brighten the room. Most of all, though, it was her singing voice they grew to love and look forward to upon waking each day and as they drifted off to sleep at night. The singing most likely violated the penance she had been set but the midwives never once chastised her.

Women birthed their babies at home. Many lived a fair distance away from the Lodge and, as many required the assistance of a midwife, there were times when all three of the midwives were called away to assist with births. At these times Yunitra found herself alone and entirely responsible for the patients and the tasks necessary to keep the Lodge operating -- often for several days.

The rumors of soldiers searching for midwives and anyone practicing the healing arts had all but disappeared from her task-filled daily life so she worked on through these times when the midwives were away with a feeling of safety. One day though, as she worked alone, she heard a commotion outside: thudding hooves, the chink of bridles and the dreaded sound of swords being unsheathed. The rumors returned to flood her mind as the door crashed open to reveal a group of soldiers brandishing swords and shouting obscenities. Patients sank down on their pallets in numb silence; their terror-filled eyes darting between Yunitra and these marauders – five of them.

One of the soldiers came to where Yunitra knelt mopping the brow of a feverish grandmother, while the others went in search of the midwives. Yunitra's hand went up towards the soldier to protect the grandmother from a possible blow. In that instant she met his eyes blazing with a lust to kill as his left arm swept down, grabbed her upraised arm, lifted her from her kneeling position and threw her against the near wall where she fell in a heap of bone-racking pain.

The soldiers, enraged at not finding the midwives they had surely been told about and encountering a girl instead, slashed at the curtains, stabbed at the patients' pallets, kicked at bowls of tinctures and herbs. Threatening to return for her and the midwives, they strode out of the Lodge. Cries from terrified patients, the sound of galloping horses receding urged her to move but her grip on wakefulness slipped to sink her into utter darkness.

Flight

She had no idea how long she had been unconscious but Yunitra's first thought on regaining consciousness was for the people in her care. This was swiftly followed by a concern for her own safety as she felt certain that the soldiers would return to carry out their threat. Should she stay and fulfill her duties to her penance and the needs of the patients or should she flee? Closing her eyes, she took a deep breath, moved one limb at a time, then struggled into a sitting position. Relief at finding she had no broken bones rushed into her slowly clearing mind as the sound of people whispering, of footfalls drawing closer to the broken battered door alerted her to move. Then, when she saw figures stepping into the Lodge, heard patients calling out greetings to their family members, not only did she feel encouraged but, also compelled to plan her escape.

She retrieved a bowl and her bundle and, like a wounded animal, crawled to and then slithered through the filthy opening at the rear of the healing room where the waste was deposited.

Fear's strength helped her sprint the hundred feet from the Lodge into the forest and she did not stop until daylight vanished and her physical strength was all but gone. An owl flew past her through a beam of moonlight streaming between treetops. This presence of an owl brought a sense of calm to her situation, and yet she also sensed a warning: *The moon may be lighting my way but it could make me more visible to anyone hunting for me.*

She darted from the shadow of a tree, through a patch of milky moonlight, to the shadow of the next tree, then through a patch of moonlight, to another tree; on and on, until suddenly she was out of the forest and in an open patch of ground. Here she had an uninterrupted view of the sky now tinted with the light of dawn. The urge to flee subsided, she sat down with her back against a tree trunk and took note of her surroundings.

Not much bigger than the interior of the lodge, the forest glade was the shape of a horseshoe edged by tall trees except at the open end of the 'horseshoe' where a stand of reeds grew in the damp earth along the bank of a stream. On the farther side of the stream the land rose to a low rounded hill. Just below the hill's crest, rays of the rising sun lit up an opening to what she hoped was a cave to shelter in. She crossed the glade, stepped into the stream, waded through knee-high water and took faltering steps up the slope. Yes, this was a cave and so, with her last strength she pitched a rock into the cave and when no sound or movement came back she entered.

The Midwives Return

Miriam was the first of the midwives to return from assisting at a birth. As she came within sight of the Lodge, the absence of smoke from the chimney alerted her. She hurried with a growing sense of there being something very wrong. When she reached the main entrance and found the door splintered and brokenly standing open, her worst fears were affirmed: the Lodge had been raided.

She came upon family members of the patients sweeping up strewn herbs and tinctures, others gathering the belongings of their loved ones in preparation of leaving the Lodge.

"Yunitra!" Yunitra? Where are you?"

When Miriam received no response, her need to restore calm and order propelled her to action. She put on a clean apron, set a fire in the hearth, added water to the cauldron, and then went to check on each patient. None had been injured by the raiders but most suffered from shock and were weak from hunger. Two of the women that had come to the aid of family members set to chopping vegetables for soup and Miriam made an herbal tea to calm all who were present.

"Please tell me what you know, what you witnessed." Miriam asked, as she handed out bowls of tea.

People shuffled, hung their heads and remained silent. Patients sank down under their covers.

"I can understand that you wish not to name or describe the invaders. But perhaps you might know the whereabouts of Yunitra. They didn't take her – did they?"

She was met with silence. Although she truly did understand the fear these humble folk were experiencing and their belief that saying nothing could keep them safe from the authorities, she was nonetheless worried about Yunitra and infuriated over the state of the Lodge that forced her to acknowledge a stark and dangerous reality. Before this day Miriam had not paid much attention to the decree declaring midwives and healers to be in the evil service of Satan and deserved to be eradicated from the earth. But now she became consumed by a deep and seething sorrow over the mindless destruction of people and their homes in the name of some new law. She believed her role in life was to continue to attend to the ill, the dying, to those giving birth and to new- born babies. She determined to continue in her commitment to her belief for as long as possible.

Some hours later that day the other two midwives, Isabella and Molly, returned from their work of assisting at births. They approached the hastily repaired entrance door to the Lodge, then, on entering, they were met with family members helping patients with preparations to depart the Lodge. They were relieved to see Miriam waving and beckoning to them to meet her at the hearth. Here, with a finger to her lips, she shook her head as a message to them to say nothing for the time being. Thankful that a soup was cooking – a soup plentiful enough to feed patients as well as their family members, the midwives, eventually, were able to sit down together at the rough-hewn plank table with their bowls of soup.

"So! They found us! Now what do we do? Fight back?" Miriam, her brow furrowed, wide fleshy shoulders hunched forward over the table, cupped her hands around her bowl of soup. Her way of coping with a situation that seemed to have spiraled away from her hold on practical realities, was to focus her worry into anger.

Isabella shifted her tall narrow body on the stool and shook her head with enough vehemence to loosen her bun of grey hair that she swatted at in irritation.

"What would be the use of fighting back – I ask you! How on earth could we do that? As women we're considered to be evil, as healers we are seen to be witches – you know that. We will be hunted until captured and what I witnessed on my return today made my blood run cold! Did you not see the state of hamlets and farms on your return today? Molly? What did you see or hear?"

Molly was the oldest and considered to be the wise one. Her snow -white hair and deeply lined face belied the wiry energy her small body emanated. Isabella and Miriam both turned to her, a gleam of hope in their eyes.

"Yes, Isabella, Miriam - by all accounts, I'd agree that we are in danger but it would be foolish to live in fear. The state of fear that people are living in now, as witnessed on my return journey, is one we cannot allow to permeate this lodge. That would only impede the healing of those who seek our help."

"Oh, Molly!" Miriam pushed away the remains of her soup. "That's all very well but the fear of which you so calmly speak has entered this lodge, has already wreaked havoc! How do you propose we diminish its presence?"

"Hush, Miriam, hush. Courage is what is called for now. I propose we tell family members to take home those of their kin who are well enough to travel. We will provide them with herbs and tinctures to take with them. And we will continue to care for those close to death or not well enough to to leave us. We have already begun to restore order here and will continue our work until the day comes – if it ever does – that we are captured."

Isabella nodded to indicate her acceptance of Molly's plan. "I expect you're right about that but have we not forgotten something or I should say: somebody?"

Molly and Miriam looked up and instantly realized. "Oh, Yunitra! How remiss of us!" Their collective sigh held a tone of frustration. Not one of them knew what to think except the worst: that Yunitra had been abducted or perhaps killed. Molly suggested they search for her belongings adding that the soldiers would not have given her the opportunity to collect her belongings if they had taken her with them. "And if they have killed her. . .?"

Isabella, expecting to find Yunitra's second shift, head cloth and tinder box found only Yunitra's sleeping mat and blanket in its customary corner. Yunitra's bundle was nowhere to be seen.

Patients, whom the three midwives questioned about the raid, had had their heads covered with bedding and therefore were not reliable witnesses. The grandmother Yunitra had been tending to when the soldiers broke down the door and burst into the lodge, recalled a soldier throwing Yunitra against the wall.

"Did she fall to the floor, Grandmother?" Miriam asked.

"Oh, she most surely did fall to the floor, the poor wee lamb."

"But, Grandmother, did she get up from the floor? Did you see if she did that?"

"No dearie, I did not see her rise up from the floor. You see I had to bury my head under the covers – it was all too awful. Do you wonder if those rotten boys - well, they are boys that think a uniform makes them into men – yes, well, those boys... They could have taken her away."

Over the following days the Lodge gradually emptied. Three patients, who wished to live out their final days in the warmth and ministrations provided by the midwives, remained.

Having agreed that a message to Yunitra's family would serve no purpose given that her parents had cast her out, the midwives resigned themselves to the loss of Yunitra from their midst. Memory of her singing and her energetic work faded into a background of quiet routine laced with strands of deep patience and a certain kind of fatalism.

Uwomo

From the time he was born, Uwomo had accompanied his parents to the vegetable gardens and orchards of a wealthy landlord for whom they worked in return for rent on their modest home. Over the years of his childhood he had grown accustomed to helping his mother and father till the fields, tend to and harvest food crops to sell at markets. However, when he turned twelve Uwomo realized he was not that interested in becoming a farmer. Having scant experience of life beyond the safe and predictable confines of the village and surrounding countryside he was unsure of what did interest him. He yearned to learn a new skill that could perhaps also provide opportunities to meet people from other parts of the country: How to go about fulfilling this need was a question that occupied most of his days and nights.

Uwomo's grandfather, a blacksmith with many years of experience in his art, noticed how restless his grandson had become. In discussion with Uwomo's parents, Grandfather suggested that Uwomo come and work with him. With his parents' blessing, Uwomo accepted Grandfather's invitation and, with relief and gratitude, he moved into Grandfather's cottage and began his time in the 'smithy' under the old man's tutelage.

Uwomo's keen interest in the demands of working close to the blazing heat of the forge, of iron heated to extreme temperatures and his natural dexterity delighted his grandfather who consistently urged him to rise to new challenges. Their reputation as a hardworking and trusted team had reached farming settlements great distances away from their village: people traveled far to have their plough shears and cooking pots mended, their knives sharpened, door hinges and hasps made and their horses shod. Almost two years of steady work went by, of companionable meals and evenings during which Grandfather's stories stirred Uwomo's imagination.

One day, Grandfather and Uwomo heard, over the roar of the fire and hammering on the anvil, a man demanding to be served. Uwomo offered to go outside to the yard to meet their visitor but Grandfather shook his head, hurriedly wiped his hands, removed his leather cap, while gesturing that Uwomo must stay out of sight. However, Uwomo's youthful curiosity got the better of him: he hid behind the half-open door from where he observed the visitor.

By Uwomo's estimation, the man's well-tailored clothes, boots of fine leather, the thoroughbred stallion he was riding, signified wealth and status. The man ignored Grandfather's greeting which angered Uwomo but he stayed put behind the half-open door. The man then ordered two women standing next to a two-wheeled cart to bring it closer to Grandfather. The women gripped the poles to which a mule or donkey was customarily harnessed, and, their faces taut with effort, began to haul the cart forward. Uwomo dashed out from behind the door into the yard to help the women move the cart.

Uwomo set down the poles of the cart at Grandfather's feet and turned to look into the cart. It was loaded with a jumble of rusted swords, daggers and shields – hundreds of neglected weapons. The man ordered Grandfather and Uwomo to unload the weapons onto the bare earth of the yard.

When the yard was all but covered with weapons and the cart was empty the man stated that repair and restoration of the contents of the cart was to begin immediately. Dismayed at the quantity and the evident neglect of the weapons, Grandfather, his manner deferential, replied that it would require at least until the spring – about two months hence - to clean and sharpen the weapons, repair the shields and armor. Grandfather's reply did not please the man who stated that the task was expected to be complete in half that time. Shouting, he ordered the women to follow with the now empty cart, kicked his horse and cantered out of the yard.

"Who is that man, Grandfather?"

"That, Uwomo, is Count Arrogar. It is he that oversees the recruitment and training of young men. . . the new ruler needs soldiers to search for midwives and herbal healers. . . Beware, Uwomo, of that man – he is not to be trusted."

The pair of them, Grandfather and Uwomo, immediately set to work on the swords, daggers, shields and armor. At times one of them would rest while the other worked alone. Uwomo, encouraged by Grandfather's trust in him and gratified to have an opportunity to prove himself, worked with care and diligence.

Finally, they accomplished the enormous task they had been ordered to complete and just in time.

On the day that Count Arrogar was expected to take delivery of the repaired weaponry, Uwomo and Grandfather rested in the yard enjoying the warmth of a spring morning as they shared a jug of ale. Idly watching a bee alighting on one blossom after another, a beam of sunlight striking the blade of a sword propped against the workshop wall with countless others jerked Uwomo up from where he was resting to walk to that sword. He remembered working on that sword, the hilt and guard, the fine and intricate engraving, the heft of the weapon.

Before Uwomo could further reflect on the possible meaning the sword in a sunbeam could signify, Count Arrogar cantered into the yard, pulling viciously on the reins to bring his horse to a stop. The animal, in a lather, blood-flecked foam around the mouth, its neck arched in protest, moved in circles breathing heavily. Uwomo approached the agitated horse, took a hold of the reins near the shank of the bit and placed his other hand on the horse's neck instantly settling the animal but arousing the Count's curiosity. Uwomo cursed himself for attracting attention, tried to divert the Count's scrutiny of him, by turning to the two women - the same two women he had helped before. This time the cart they pulled was loaded with firewood: payment for work on the weaponry.

Uwomo assisted the women with unloading and stacking the logs. He then loaded the repaired weaponry into the empty cart. Although he and the women had not spoken, he sensed an undercurrent of fear in their averted eyes. *Are they warning me of some impending trouble?*

Like a predator stalking its prey the Count licked his thin lips, stroked his moustache as he observed Uwomo's broad muscled shoulders, strong arms, capable hands, deft fingers. With narrowed eyes moving down Uwomo's torso, the Count noted strength in long thighs, sure-footedness and a powerful grace in the fluid movement of Uwomo's body as he

loaded the cart. Unaware of the Count's assessment of him and therefore not suspicious of the man's motives, Uwomo experienced a burst
of surprise when the Count ordered him to select a weapon for himself
from the hundreds he and Grandfather had restored. His youthful pride
leading him, Uwomo selected, with undisguised pleasure, the sword that
had shone in a sunbeam earlier that morning. The Count took note of
this and, before riding away, he ordered Uwomo to report to the training
ground for recruits at the barracks in three day's time and to bring the
sword with him.

Training

Uwomo reported to the training grounds at the barracks three days later. He did this out of a fear of the cruel treatment that would be inflicted on his family such as the evivtion from their home , for instance, or the termination of their work for the landlord if he disobeyed the Count's orders.

At the training grounds he joined a line of slow-moving young men, his mind troubled with how he could reconcile pride at owning a magnificent sword with the wrenching loss of Grandfather's company and the work he had grown to love.

Count Arrogar assessed each recruit from a throne-like seat on a raised platform. Two bodyguards stood at attention on either side of the Count. At the Count's feet and spread to the left and right of him was an array of shields. One by one the recruits halted at the raised platform and waited to be handed a shield. Once the Count had pointed out a shield he deemed suitable for a recruit, a bodyguard would hand it to the aspiring soldier saying: "You will earn your sword in good time." When Uwomo came to the platform and was handed an ornately engraved shield of considerable weight, he heard the Count say: "You, young pup, have a sword. Put it and this shield to good use and you will be given a horse."

Powerless to reverse the situation in which he found himself Uwomo vowed to keep his distance from the Count. He also made two decisions: to form no friendships with fellow recruits and to excel in the face of any challenge he met. To become an undefeated warrior he trained his body to endure extreme physical exertion and his mind to razor-sharp focus. This did not escape the Count's notice and, as promised, Uwomo was soon given a horse to train: a stallion with a coat the color of smoke and clouds with a loyal and stout heart. Uwomo named his horse Maximus.

Uwomo and Maximus became companions and also forged a strong bond of trust that ultimately turned them into a ruthless unit on battlefields and on raids of villages. This bond sufficed to quell any yearning Uwomo felt for the life he had left behind him; yearning, he told himself, weakens a man.

Over time he also mastered the art of self-deception by repeatedly reminding himself that discipline of his body and shutting away feelings of tenderness would keep his family safe and improve his skills. But, by deceiving himself this way, his empathy for humanity began to diminish.

However, to his loyal and sturdy companion, Maximus, Uwomo communicated an unswerving love and trust. Tales of the warrior and his smoke-grey steed, their swift and exacting methods, traveled from villages to hamlets, to market places and grew to heroic proportions with each telling. Uwomo heard of these tales and knew he was expected to enjoy being revered and feared, but his lust for battle plagued his sense of decency that Grandfather had exemplified.

Waking from yet another night of restless thoughts and an increasing sense of reaching the limits of his forbearance with his life, he and four soldiers readied their horses and left the barracks armed and ready to carry out a raid of a village.

Uwomo led the four soldiers to the top of a hill from where they familiarized themselves with the layout of the village in the valley below. Something about the village tugged at his memory: the layout with a blacksmith's workshop on the outskirts, the familiarity of houses facing a square. A surge of horror gripped his bowels as the realization that this was the village where he had been born; the very place where he had worked with Grandfather. He could not. . . would not raid this village.

Forced now, to admit to how close he had come to raiding his birthplace and his family, to how inured he had become to the suffering of others, he and Maximus moved to the side of the road as he signaled to the soldiers to proceed ahead. The four soldiers drew their swords and proceeded at full gallop down the slope to the sleeping village.

Uwomo and Maximus wheeled about and galloped away towards a deep forest where he hoped they could hide from detection. Throughout that day as they fled, Uwomo repeatedly asked himself this question: *Could I have stopped the raid?*

And to the steady drumming of Maximus' hooves the answer Uwomo received was No.

Raid

Morning sunlight shrouded by a film of dense acrid smoke cast a ghostly pall over village inhabitants huddled in the market square. Children buried their faces in the folds of women's skirts to avoid inhaling the smoke. Women covered their mouths and noses with their shawls. They glared at the soldiers from eyes glassy with shock and hatred. A few sons, fathers and grandfathers who had not been injured while protecting their kin, hung their heads as if the weight of their grief was too much to bear. Women, children and men - overcome with the loss of their homes that were now heaps of smoldering thatch and crumbled walls - experienced a sense of defeat hitherto unknown to them. How were they going to rebuild? And when would they be allowed to retrieve their goats and chickens that had scattered into the surrounding countryside? The entire village was in ruins. The dead lay where they had fallen. Vultures circled overhead.

The four soldiers, pleased with the destruction they had wreaked, were openly gloating despite not having found a healer or midwife in the village. They were making ready to return to the barracks where they would report to Count Arrogar when one soldier noticed that their fifth man, their leader was missing.

"Where are Uwomo and Maximus?" asked a soldier. "We dare not return to barracks without our leader. Where is he?"

"Uh, he was there at the crest of the hill... he told us to go ahead – remember?" "We entered this godforsaken hellhole ahead of him." Replied another.

"What are you saying? He went where, then?" demanded the first soldier.

"Just that. I did see him but . . . "

"We'll have to search the surrounding area. Curse that man! But, then. . . he and his horse could be dead."

"Pah! Nobody has the strength or speed to do that- kill Uwomo or that stallion of his. . . and not one of these pathetic excuses for humanity in this village is able!"

"True enough. So what do we do now? Search for him on our way back to barracks?"

"We had better do that – search for him before we report to Count Arrogar. There's nothing more to do here – time to go."

"No, not yet - not before we have threatened this lot with the fires of hell and damnation if any one of them is caught harboring even one of those cursed healer women. Then we will ride out."

The four soldiers formed a line facing the huddled villagers and in unison declared:

"Today you have met the wrath of the new god. Be warned, we will return if we hear that any of you is hiding a healer, a midwife or any person foolish enough to disobey the decree. Go bury your dead before vultures feast on their eyeballs."

The soldiers cantered away.

Once the the soldiers were out of earshot a murmur of voices punctuated with coughing and sobs of despair grew to a dull roar of collective outrage as villagers dispersed to prepare the dead for burial. One of the Elder women, Manona, on hearing the name "Uwomo" during the soldiers' exchange about their missing leader, felt great relief that her son, Uwomo, had no part in the raid.

Although Manona had not laid eyes on Uwomo since the day he was recruited, she had held an unwavering belief that one day he would leave the world of battle and live in gentle peace.

At the grave of Uwomo's father whom she had buried an hour ago, she blessed the grave and also that of Grandfather who had died the year before. She then added a thought of blessing to her son. The grief that had engulfed her like a suffocating cover of wet hide over her soul, now had an edge lifted enough to allow some light and air to enter.

The soldiers' mission to search for their leader took a scant few minutes as they made a cursory scan of the horizon. In truth, the four men were more interested in getting back to the barracks for a jug of ale and a bowl of meat stew with bread..

Once the horses were stabled the four soldiers went directly to the eating hall where Cook stood over a cauldron of stewing meat. The ale in jugs stood invitingly on the long board table. Spooning food into their mouths, washing this down with ale, they were unaware of whispered questions passing between other soldiers seated at the long table: "Where's Uwomo?" and "There's no sign of Maximus in the stable".

Cook, averse to the spread of contagious fear and uncertainty, confronted the four men. "So, tell us now; where is your leader? I see that you have not saved a seat for him at the table. Word from the stables is that Maximus also, appears to be missing. What happened out there today?"

The four soldiers cringed under Cook's steely glare while feigning a lack of concern. "Who knows?" one soldier quipped: "He could be whiling away his time – delaying his return. In any case, the Count will not be ready for the day's report of our successful mission – he'll be with his wine for a while. We have time to eat and drink. And uh wait for Uwomo."

"And we all know, don't we?" another soldier declared while wiping his mouth on a sleeve – "how the Count favors that man of few words, that stand- alone unfriendly man – Uwomo."

Cook pulled himself up to his full height, his prodigious belly a threatening bulge. "Your leader is not one that 'whiles away his time' . . . A man of few words he is, I grant you that, but a finer warrior I've yet to meet in all these years I've fed you lot." Cook turned on his heel, making for the stove, and growled: "I don't like this situation and I swear the Count will like it even less."

Report

Cook's words had silenced the clatter of spoons, the rumble of voices that customarily filled the large hall. The quiet, heavy with foreboding, unnerved the four soldiers; they felt the chill of it and hurried to finish their meal. But they were not quick enough. The Count's bodyguards – a pair of burly men that accompanied the Count everywhere he went - entered the hall. They demanded that those who had accompanied Uwomo, rise to identify themselves. Everybody stopped eating. Nobody turned to look at the pair of bodyguards for fear of making eye contact with them. The four soldiers stood to attention then heard the order they had been dreading.

"To the Count's quarters immediately! His lordship awaits an explanation."

Count Arrogar, a flagon of wine at hand, his tall slender body, feminine in its shapeliness about the hips, lounged on cushions near to a crackling fire in the hearth. He stroked his moustache, patted at his sweating forehead with a lace-edged handkerchief. An odor of perfumed sweat and stale breath over- rode the smell of beeswax candles.

"What is this I hear about you four returning to barracks without your leader?"

"Your Lordship. The mission we carried out today was highly successful. Engaged as we were in the complete destruction of a village. . . Uh, busy as we were, sir, the absence of our leader was not noticed until we had rounded up the inhabitants – those still living, sir. Upon awaiting our leader's command to depart we discovered he and his horse, Maximus, were not present, sir."

The Count placed the flagon on a nearby table with a trembling hand. As he moved to sit upright, his body seemed to uncoil like a viper ready to strike. "Not present? Not present! Are you telling me that he disappeared?"

"Your Lordship our first thought was that he could be dead. . . "

"Dead!" The Count shrieked. "Who, in this kingdom, this land, I ask you, has the strength, speed and skill to kill Uwomo?"

"Sir – yes, we asked the same question but do not know what else could have happened to him."

The Count paled with the effort to control a surge of jagged rage at the thought of losing his prize warrior. And not only that, but Uwomo's presence in the barracks had provided the Count with a vicarious pleasure and appreciation for the man's handsome strength. Sheer hatred of his prize warrior for causing these unpleasant emotions then rose to fill his gorge causing him to sputter into his wine goblet.

The four soldiers hung their heads, stared at their boots to avoid being party to the Count's embarrassing show of feelings for Uwomo and to hide their guilt over not carrying out a thorough search for their leader.

When the Count had regained a semblance of composure, he filled his goblet with wine, emptied it in gulps and heaved himself off the cushions to stand facing the four soldiers and his bodyguards.

"At daybreak you will be ready to ride out with me. We will conduct a relentless search for Uwomo and Maximus. We will continue until we find him. And when we find him we will kill him and his horse. We will kill them slowly and painfully. Prepare for an extended time away. Ask Cook to provide you with rations. Leave me now."

Desertion

Uwomo had lost all sense of how long or far he had been walking. With each plodding step, waves of shock snapped along his spine, jerked his lowered head to face forward. His mind relentlessly returned to that moment when he knew that he would cease fighting for the new law; the same moment in which he and Maximus had galloped away from his home village. And now, his legs about to give way under him, he was forced to stop walking. It was then that he noticed a flat-topped rock on the side of the path and, with a resigned grunt, sat down on it. With elbows on his knees, his fisted hands under his chin, he supported his head of matted hair and stared at his blood-stained boots. Cries from dying people, whimpers of the trapped and terrified assailed his thoughts. It occurred to him that he may have left the clash and clamor of battlefields and village raids but the sounds and smells of death and fear seemed lodged in his very being.

Although certain that Count Arrogar would mount a relentless search for him and Maximus, he felt no misgiving for Uwomo had come to accept that he would rather be hunted than continue to live the way he had for the past seven years. Yes, he would be branded a coward, a deserter, and, if he and Maximus were ever found, Uwomo knew that both he and his horse would be tortured before they were put to death. He determined then, to elude capture at whatever cost.

But where is Maximus?

He lowered his hands to his knees, shook his head as if this could dislodge the roaring in his mind and recalled tethering Maximus to a tree . . . *what did I then do and where. . . oh heaven, help me. . .*

He studied his knuckles, the traceries of scars and thickened veins that fanned like a map of effort along his forearms. Turning over his hands he looked at calloused palms, a pang of missing the feel of the reins and his horse's quick response triggering questions he had not asked himself before: *Why had men, for centuries, obeyed authorities that trained them to kill? And kill they did. Could obeying orders be tied into striving . . . for what though? Honor?*

What honor is there in killing defenseless people in their homes? Surely there must be other ways a man can be honorable? Grandfather taught me that respect fosters honor; respect of self and other. . . did my blind obedience to the authorities replace my self-respect?

Little by little, a scent of salt and seaweed mixed with wild herbs and sun-warmed earth penetrated his troubled mind. He sniffed the air, inhaled deeply and, as he exhaled, a twinge of pain in the center of his chest increased to an excruciating intensity. Groaning, he unclasped his cloak flung it off his shoulders onto the rock and, fingers scrabbling at the clasp of his padded vest, he pulled it open and away from his chest. Panting with urgency, his hand moved over his heart searching for the source of the pain and there encountered the hilt of his war sword; its blade embedded in his chest.

He stood, braced his legs against the rock, gripped the hilt, tightened shoulder and arm muscles, inhaled and on an explosive exhale he pulled the sword out in a single mighty effort of will.

The blade, slippery with his blood, pierced the air as he pointed his sword at the sky howling: What use am I now? What will I do as a non-combatant?

He cried out for mercy and fell backwards onto the rock. The sword slipped from his grasp, dropped to the ground.

A playful race of waves became a mild swell farther from shore. Rich hues of dusk fanned across the western sky.

That he had allowed himself to become as vulnerable as he was now: lying on his back on a rock, his sword beyond his reach, his chest bared and eyes open to the sky, gave him pause. *I've witnessed the surrender of many people – far too many – but my own surrender? No. This is new to me.*

Drained from the effort of struggling to recollect the whereabouts of Maximus, he wished for oblivion but, instead, he re-directed his inward search to look outwards to the heavens where a night sky, replete with swathes of sparkling stars seemed to be waiting for his attention. And, as if somewhere out there, in the vastness, there could be an answer to his plea, he whispered: "*Oh, heaven help me! I abandoned my loyal companion, Maximus and cannot remember where that was. Help me remember!*"

As if in response to his plea Uwomo saw himself removing saddle, bridle and battle armor from his horse, hurling these into the middle of a fast-flowing river together with his helmet and shield, Maximus turning to him with a questioning nicker and a nudge as if to say: *What are we doing here?*

Uwomo's memory cleared and he recalled leading Maximus to a secluded area in a forest down river from where he had hurled their battle gear and . . . oh, yes! *I tethered him to a tree . . . the tie rope was long enough for him to reach the river nearby but also to allow him to shelter in the trees. I did leave him with food, didn't I? Ah, the nosebag of grains and a pile of sweet hay.*

And then?

He had walked away from Maximus. He had continued walking and walking, blindly crashing through forest undergrowth; forcing the pain of separation down and away from his mind until he had come to this hillside and to this flat-top rock.

At least he had set his horse free. But what of him self; was he free?

The gentle rhythm of waves washing over pebbles, like a lullaby, soothed him to sleep. He dreamed of cradling a baby in his arms, of leaning into the caress of a kind and tender woman, of providing sustenance and support, of learning to love and to be loved.

Sanctuary

Thankful that the interior of the cave was clean and unoccupied, Yunitra gingerly lay down facing the entrance. Sleep overtook her and although sporadically disturbed by fear-filled memories, exhaustion, like a drug, held her motionless until a thirst for water woke her.

She stepped from the cave entrance into a gentle quiet evening. There on the farther bank of the stream was the glade edged in a semi circle by the dark trees of the forest. Recognition of these simple landmarks were comforting and encouraged her to set off with her bowl down the hill to the stream. She dipped her bowl into a small pool where the stream curled and eddied around a boulder and drank the clear sweet water, then stepped into the pool and lay down, her feet anchored to the boulder. The stream washed over and around her bruised head, cascaded over her shoulders and poured over her breasts and belly, thighs and shins cleansing the filth of her escape. Despite the soothing sound and feel of the stream she worried that by fleeing from the lodge, she had abandoned the ill and infirm in her care, had shirked responsibilities the elder woman had depended on her to carry out.

An immediate need for food now overlaid her troubled conscience, urged her to explore the area surrounding the cave. She found berries, ate these as she foraged for other edible foods: mushrooms and leafy plants. When she discovered wild parsnips and carrots she fashioned a digging stick to unearth these edible roots but then realized that they would taste far better when cooked. Dare she build a fire to cook the roots? A small one surely would not alert anybody searching for her and if she contained the fire in the mouth of the cave during daylight hours. . . the longing for warm food decided her.

She selected stones from the stream as if each was a new companion, then arranged these in a fire ring at the entrance to the cave. Her head

31

cloth served as a sling in which to carry twigs and dry branches. She put her tinderbox to use and soon the kindling caught alight. The roots she had foraged cooked perfectly on the hot stones. With each mouthful she could feel her strength returning and in some way the warmth of the fire soothed the lonely place within her.

Most days were spent creating as much comfort as possible: foraging for food, collecting kindling and logs for the fire and picking fern fronds and tall grasses for a bed. Her nights, infused by the distant sound of the stream provided deep restful sleep unless memories of recent terror or the loss of companionship disturbed her. As an escaped penitent, the irony of her silent and lonely existence was not lost on her. That nobody seemed to be searching for her increased her relief at not having been discovered, but the possibility that nobody actually cared about her was hard to bear.

To allay the hollowness these contemplations caused, she paid attention to the songs of a variety of birds that filled the air at sunrise and sunset. The throaty call of a coal-black raven further added to a sense of companionship. On most evenings, it swooped down to perch on a nearby rock like an ancient sentinel, to observe Yunitra's fire-making and food preparation.

Gradually, as her daily existence became a pattern she relied upon, a shift in the content of her thoughts was occurring: a brightening of confidence, a trust in her self, a change in attitude. She continued to perform her daily rituals of waking with the dawn, bathing in the stream, foraging for food, freshening her bed, eating at the fire, with a sense of enjoyment that surprised her.

However, at the first signs of Autumn: cooler nights, leaves on some trees turning gold, morning dew heavy on the grass, she was forced to address the question of her survival in the coming months of winter.

Oh, Mama you could at least have provided me with a shawl!

A Fallen Soldier

One morning, daydreaming in autumn sunlight on a sun-warmed rock near the stream, an almost forgotten sound of the chink of a bridle and steady hoof beats forced Yunitra to pay attention. Fear snaked through her. She crouched down behind a stand of reeds poised to flee and watched the trees at the edge of the glade from where a horse emerged and entered the glade at a slow walk, its rider slumped over in the saddle.

The horse came to a stop, the rider tilted sideways then fell to the ground with a dull thud. He lay there on his back, his arms flung wide as if he had been flung. The horse moved to graze on the lush green grass at stream's edge.

Taut with anxiety, her eyes fixed on the prone body she watched for movement. Seeing none, not even a flicker of eyelids, she approached the fallen body that appeared to be a young soldier not too much older than she. His sword sheathed in an ornate scabbard, was held in place by a leather belt at his hips. Across his broad chest, an embroidered bib covered a padded vest. . . *ah! It is the insignia of the soldiers fighting for the new law. . . oh, no!*

Curiosity compelled her to step closer, to look at his face. The horse continued to graze close by, unconcerned by her presence which calmed her long enough to take in the face of the soldier: a high forehead, a strong blade of a nose, shapely lips, dark eyebrows forming two arcs over wide-set eyes now closed and deeply sunk into their sockets. Then she noticed a fresh scar running from his jawline up to matted ink-black curls over his temple.

A desire to touch him, to stroke his forehead, apply balm to that scar, flamed through her. Instead, she cushioned his head with fallen leaves, gently, almost lovingly drew together the edges of his cloak she could reach without waking him and covered his tall muscled body before stepping away to stand behind the horse's shoulder to observe the man from a safer distance.

The horse felt her nearness, tossed its smoke-grey forelock and turned its head towards her with a reassuring glance before returning to graze. Yunitra stroked its shoulder and broad powerful chest as if to impart some of the loving kindness tingling in her arms. She then filled her bowl with water and placed this within the sleeping soldier's reach.

Introspection slowed her return to the cave, caused her to look back at the clearing many times as if fixing the tableaux of a fallen soldier and his grey charger at peace in her world. Could his appearance be Providence at work rather than a threatening invasion? Perhaps he had not come to harm her but to help her in some way she did not yet know?

An element of fear remained though. Could he even be the one who had flung her against the wall of the healing room? If she had seen into this soldier's eyes today she would have known if it were indeed the one who had flung her. She would not forget the eyes that blazed at her that time. And, if it were that one, what would be her wisest course of action now?

Unlike fear, a new sensation as tender as a seedling reaching for the light, quivered through her body. A strange lethargy mixed with a heightened state of awareness confused and perplexed her, dulled her appetite. Instead of making a fire she retreated to the back of the cave to lie down on her bed of ferns and grasses.

Dreams of hope and fear intermingled through the night; images of blazing eyes and an arm poised to strike interwove with the poignant peace she had witnessed in the glade. Sunrise brought to her no further clarity. On her familiar path down the hill to the stream, she told herself to be cautious, to take no precipitous course of action, to ask no questions that could endanger her but soldier and horse were gone. The only sign of their having been present was a pile of horse dung and an area of flattened leaves and grasses where the man had lain, and her emptied bowl. Assailed by a mixture of disappointment, frustration and sheer relief, she retrieved her bowl and trudged up the slope to the cave.

I so wanted the soldier and his horse to be there this morning. Am I so lonely that even a possibility of danger has not extinguished these new feelings that soldier awoke in me?

She stood at the mouth of the cave looking in at the home she had created and saw her existence from a changed point of view. Her second shift and head-cloth neatly folded at the head of her bed of fern fronds and grasses seemed to give off a sense of futility. The emptiness of her bowl began an ache in her belly. *He drank from my bowl. . .*

The stones of her fire-ring brought a flicker of purpose that quickly died.

She paced back and forth at the cave entrance, then ran down the slope, stormed into the clearing and stood howling like a wolf. Onto the faint outline of the soldier's body she lay down and wept. She wept over the wasting of love by those who killed the healers. She sobbed over the loss of love that caused her parents to betray her. Eventually, her grief and sorrow spent, her loving heart eased, she surrendered to the earth beneath her, the sky over her and drifted into a deep dreamless sleep in the glade.

The day progressed from a morning that had seen her drift into sleep, through the sun's zenith and into an afternoon of gathering clouds and shifting winds. It was a gust of cold wind and a rain-filled cloud covering the sun that stirred her to get up from the ground and to make her way back to the cave. The companionable whispers of the tall grasses she had come to know now sounded to her like malevolent hisses. The stream, reflecting a steel grey sky, seemed to resent her wading through it. Even her daily visitor, the raven, eyed her with seeming suspicion.

Sitting at the fire, chewing food, she stared into flames reflected in a quivering curtain of rain water falling from the upper lip of the cave entrance. At her back the cave's deep darkness breathed calm.

A while later, she curled up on her fern frond bed, faced the dying fire and concentrated on what she could possibly do about the onset of winter as well as the raw feelings she was left with after her emotional storm in the glade that had bared her soul to an inexplicable yearning.

Perhaps I should find my way home to my parents?

That possibility only served to cause a clamoring in Yunitra's mind as she imagined the punishments she would receive for escaping her penance and abandoning the people in her care. No, she was certain she would not be welcomed home.

In that case I have no alternative. I must leave this sweet place before winter sets in. But in which direction should I go? The sun rises over there from where I fled through the forest to this place. . . Ah, I have not once ventured to the top of the knoll — the roof of this cave - neither have I faced in the direction of where the sun sets. . .

Decision

At sunrise Yunitra packed her tinderbox, bowl and second shift into her head cloth that she had fashioned into a sling bag and climbed to the crest of the knoll. Feeling as naked as a new-born bird, she tried, in vain, to ignore a longing for the protection the cave had provided; tried to shut out the soothing voice of the stream, the songs of her bird companions celebrating a night of rain.

I must bid this place farewell. . . I will not look back.

But by looking forwards what she saw caused a tremor of shock: smoke and flames in the distance rose towards clouds glowering over a vast expanse of barren earth. Down from where she stood, a fair distance away, people – most of whom appeared to be women, children and the elderly - moved in a slow shuffling plod along a road that crossed the land before her. Ahead of the straggling line, rode a foursome of mounted soldiers, their banners limp in the thick air. At the tail end of the line of people, rode two horsemen, whips at rest across their thighs.

Curious about where they were going and why, she was about to run down the hill towards them when a sliver of anxiety held her firmly on the crest of the knoll. Three women, breaking out of the line of people, were going to the aid of a person stumbling, to others who had fallen, to a woman carrying a baby. Something about the way these three women moved, the way they appeared to be ignoring the soldiers struck Yunitra like a blow to her stomach as recognition flooded her mind. *Isabella? Molly? Miriam? Oh, no! Does this mean the Lodge was raided again and the soldiers found you? Mama? Papa? Are you in that line of people? If you are, then by banishing me my life was saved. . . am I indebted to you? No. I saved my own life by fleeing the Lodge. I may be a fugitive but I am alive. . .*

By the time the people and soldiers were far enough away from where she crouched, her state of aloneness had ballooned into a litany of 'what ifs', perceived losses and just plain fear. As she was reaching for the memory of the three midwives and their calm wisdom that she now sorely needed, her mother's chiding voice over- rode Yunitra's focus: *Oh, Yunitra! Look at what you've done now!* This almost extinguished her faltering courage but not quite.

The barren land before her cringed under a ceiling of bruised clouds, caused an outburst of: *Done? I? Mama? I could ask you to tell me what **you** have done Mama — yes, you and Father banished me — you did! I see no good reason to listen to you ever again.*

Admonishing her mother may have served to reinstate Yunitra's courage but it did also make her wonder at the impetus driving her to stay true to a quest about which she felt utterly ignorant.

Beyond the lifeless expanse of unyielding hostility, a distant horizon bathed in a gentle light came into view. As an incentive to traverse the wasteland, she kept that horizon in sight and set off from the knoll.

In sharp contrast to the protected sanctuary in which she had recently lived, this landscape offered no place to rest, no shade during days of searing heat, no shelter during bitterly cold nights. Afraid to light a fire, even if there were twigs to burn, Yunitra kept moving through night and day. She sorely missed her cave, her fern-frond bed and the enclosed protection of a solid rock wall to lean against.

Finally, she came to a standstill when her battle against fatigue and despair could no longer be won. As soon as she did that, a scent of water reached her. She sniffed the air, narrowed her eyes and saw, ahead of her, what appeared to be a lone tree casting a circle of shade on white sand. Skeptical that the tree would not be real but a mirage or perhaps a figment of her imagination, she nevertheless walked towards it.

To her amazement rather than shifting as a mirage would, the tree took on an increasing substance of aliveness. The crown of wide spreading branches with lacy leaves created that circle of shade she now stepped into.

Embracing the slender tree trunk, she cooled her cheeks on its satiny bark, then sank down onto the soft sand. Beneath her, a tired and silent earth breathed. Leafy branches above her whispered but, within her, an entity stirred.

A throbbing pain over her eyes caused her to sit up and place a hand on her forehead as if checking for a fever. Pressure in the center of her forehead intensified until she felt it would erupt. Driven by a force not her own, she braced her body against the tree trunk and plunged the forefinger of her right hand directly into the center of her forehead. Here her finger encountered something alive. She brought her thumb to meet her forefinger and grabbed a hold of whatever was lodged in there. Tightening her grip, she began to tug. On the first few tugs she felt a resistance then, suddenly, it gave way and out came a long sinuous body; its flat head tightly gripped between her thumb and forefinger. She extended a trembling arm away from her side to inspect this entity. Writhing in convulsive surges, she watched it in awe as it transformed into a serpent; a serpent with black diamond-shaped markings outlined in gold and scarlet. Ivory colored scales along the full length of its underside gleamed. The serpent's eyes, the color of topaz, regarded her with cool calm.

Yunitra released the serpent at the base of the tree from where it slithered up the trunk to a branch around which it coiled like an elaborate bracelet in sun- speckled shade. Giddy with elation over having freed the source of pain and also depleted of all her physical strength, she leaned against the tree trunk to steady the tremble in her legs. Into the ensuing sense of peace and quiet, her mother's voice intruded with a warning of the dire outcomes that would befall Yunitra if she ever consorted with the serpent. "Serpents, Yunitra, are evil and no good girl shows any interest in these vile creatures. Keep this in mind: Adam and Eve were forbidden to eat from the Tree of Knowledge in the Garden of Eden . . . it was the serpent that tempted them to eat the forbidden fruit. They couldn't withstand the temptation, - yes, *temptation* Yunitra!- Adam and Eve ate from the Tree of Knowledge and, of course, were punished. Yes, punished! Yunitra and well deserved it was. You will do well to remember this: they were banished from the Garden of Eden to live out their lives in a barren desert."

Even as a young child Yunitra had been unwilling to heed her mother's warning or to accept the story of Adam and Eve's punishment. Now, she became even more convinced that humans and creatures shared a natural world and could live co-operatively within it.

The band of light on the horizon that had drawn her from the knoll above the cave; that had spurred her to cross the wasteland, resurfaced in her mind as a kindly replacement for her mother's dire warnings thus encouraging her to find a way to reach that light. She would need to climb the tree to gain a clearer view.

The serpent took no notice of her as she climbed past the branch on which it was coiled. From the uppermost branches she could now see over a steep rise of black lava rocks, a most welcoming sight: a beach of golden sand lapped by sparkling ocean waves in a small protected bay.

It was not difficult to come down from the top of the tree but negotiating the steep incline of lava rock turned out to be more demanding of her strength than she had thought. The glimpse of a bay and sparkling ocean from the tree-top urged her to reach it. She crawled, clambered and dragged her tired body up and then, finally, to the summit and down the other side.

As her feet touched soft powdery sand, she flung the sling bag to the side, ran across the beach, threw herself into the water to float on her back with her eyes open to a blue cloudless sky. All she could feel and think about was a deep gratitude mixed with a keen sense of having accomplished an important step in her life. Precisely what that step signified remained a mystery to her but the realness of where she now found herself seemed enough for the time being.

Eventually waves carried her to shore to deposit her with a purposeful nudge towards dry sand. She sat up and began to pay attention to her surroundings.

A Horse

The crest of land from where Yunitra had climbed down to the sand, curved in a jumble of rocks into the water to the left of her. In front of her the wide ocean. To her right, at the far end of the bay, a grassy green finger of land – a headland - contoured with steeply sided gullies - jutted out into the ocean.

With the sling bag over her shoulder, she set off along the beach towards that headland. Cliffs to her right rose vertically from the sandy beach. Grasses growing along the top edges of the cliffs high above her appeared as a green fringe sparkling with sun-filled drops of dew. She drank sweet fresh water trickling from clefts in the cliff- face.

Farther along at the shoreline on her left, rocks glimmered in the wash and splash of waves careening over and drawing back from their black craggy surfaces. Pelicans perched on high points of the rocks held their wings open to dry, their breasts facing the sun.

That headland drew her like a magnet. One moment it was clearly visible in its vivid green-ness and, in the next, concealed in billows of ocean mist.

During one of the moments when the mist cleared she thought she saw a horse standing absolutely still on the crest of the headland; so still that she believed it to be a stone statue. . . until it raised its head to sniff the air.

Yunitra scrambled over tufted grass, jumped from from one moss-covered boulder to the next to reach the horse observing her with keen interest. Only when she was within touching distance did the horse lower its head to greet her. In a bright flash of recognition, a shout of joy escaped her as she wrapped her arms about its neck.

The horse nuzzled her shoulder, blew bursts of breath into her hair all the while nickering from deep in its belly. She pressed her cheek to its

41

muzzle, stroked its neck and crooned with a happiness she had not experienced for far too long.

Eventually she pulled away to look at the horse from a calmer state of mind. Its massive ribcage showed through an unkempt smoke-grey coat. Sunken pockets above the eyes indicated hunger and neglect. Except for a tattered length of rope hanging loosely about its neck, it bore nothing: no saddle, no bridle – not even a feedbag.

Oh, no – what happened to you? Where's your rider?

Cleansing

As dawn tinged the sky with shades of rose and apricot, Uwomo stirred on the flat-top rock where he had fallen asleep. As his dream faded, the source of his self-loathing ballooned from the depths of where he had successfully buried it during his life as a fighting man. Disgust rose to his gorge, caused him to sit up. Widening his eyes, he bent forward to vomit onto the ground. Disgorged bile pooled between his blood- stained boots while he faced the possibility that he had plundered seven years of his life by obeying orders to kill.

An attempt to cope with the ache of missing Maximus and an immense sadness, he resorted to activity by taking off his boots, his padded vest and his belt. These he dropped on the ground near the rock. The stench of him spurred him to get down to the water to wash. He stepped out of his frayed trousers, rolled these, his tunic shirt and loincloth into a bundle. Should he also wash his cloak? And what about cleaning the sword blade? No, he thought: better to leave his cape on the rock and his boots next to his sword and padded vest.

Sunlight licked at his bare skin, at his battle scars, at the one on his cheek. A sea breeze teased at his scrotum, cooled his arm -pits. He spread his toes, rose on the balls of his feet and careened through the tall grasses down the hillside to the shore where he dropped the bundled clothes on his way to hurling him self into the ocean. Salty water soaked his skin like a balm, urged him to flex muscles, stretch limbs to their full extent and to float effortlessly on his back.

Buoyancy seemed to envelope and also carry him. His mother's voice reached his thoughts as an ocean swell rose to become a wave that carried him to shore. The instant his body slithered over the pebbles on the beach he understood without being able to explain it, that, yes, he first experienced this feeling when leaving his mother's womb. That dream image of cradling a baby in his arms flickered through his mind and he snatched at it just in time to remember a larger part of the dream: of longing to soothe loneliness, of wanting to know the tender caress of a kind woman, of the desire to learn how to sustain life with love.

He collected his stinking clothes, returned to the water, got these soaking wet before rubbing, wringing, beating them on pebbles, rinsing and wringing again and again. His actions became frantic with a feverish need to cleanse him self of all past activities, every shred of pain he inflicted, every tear he had brought to the eyes of those he had harmed. Not once did he stop to wonder if his memories could also be thus cleansed. He then spread out his clothes to dry and returned to the water to wash his hair and to scrub his body

Reunion

The horse responded to Yunitra's question with a nudge to her shoulder then set off on a narrow path along the edge of a cliff that eventually brought them to a meadow that sloped down to a beach of pebbles and sparkling water.

Here Yunitra stood stock still, her hand on the horse's shoulder to take in the scene before her: waves washing onto a shore of pebbles, clothing drying on stones, a naked man cavorting in the water, shouting unintelligible words. The horse blew a snort into her hair and trotted down the hillside towards the man; tail swishing, mane streaming in the ocean breeze, its excited nickers riding the air.

Uwomo, thigh-deep in water, bent from the waist to rinse his hair. Out of the corner of his eye a movement at the shoreline caused him to swiftly raise his head while he cursed himself for being in such an unguarded state. His hand blindly felt for his sword, found his naked hip instead so he turned to face whatever it was that had entered his peripheral vision.

He pushed his dripping wet hair away from his face. A horse? Yes, unmistakably so. It stood at the water's edge a few paces from him, near his clothes drying on stones. A horse, high in the shoulder, broad across the chest, swishing its tail, mane rippling in the sea breeze; a horse with a coat the color of smoke and clouds.

Maximus!

Uwomo splashed his way out of the water shouting, sobbing, questioning, rejoicing and threw his arms about the horse's neck. Maximus snorted, nibbled at Uwomo's shoulder, nickered and then raised his great head to release a jubilant neigh that seemed to shake the heavens.

Lost And Found

Transfixed for some minutes by the exuberant exchange between horse and naked man, Yunitra then suddenly felt awkward and conspicuous as if their meeting were some private communication she should not be observing. Behind her a flat-topped rock that looked to be suitable to sit on took her gaze away from the beach but there was a cloak spread over the rock. She lifted a corner of the cloak, sniffed and recoiled at the smell of sweat mingled with blood, traces of horse overlaid with a weary staleness. As if it were about to scald her, she pulled away her hand, turned and there, on the ground next to the rock was a pair of blood-stained boots, a padded vest, a leather belt, an unsheathed sword.

A tremor of fear raised the hair on the back of her neck. The owner of these items on and near the rock appeared to be a soldier - a fighting man. That must be him with the horse. . . she and the horse had recognized each other back there on the headland. . .

To help her decide on her next step she turned to reassess the situation of horse and man on the beach. In so doing, her foot knocked the sword against the rock causing the fine tempered blade to ring like a struck gong. The shouting and neighing, abruptly ceased.

The naked man in the shallows with his arms around the neck of the smoke-grey horse pulled away from the embrace and stared at the figure standing near that rock. The horse turned to also stare. Despite the distance of a few hundred yards between her and the man with a horse, she felt pinned by the dual scrutiny.

His guttural shout of "Who are you?" broke the spell as he sprinted to his clothes drying on stones.

Torn between the urge to flee and a need to stay in order to know more, a sunlit glade on a golden autumn day, a warhorse, his warrior tumbling to the leaf-strewn ground, his inert body and oh, the deep sensations that had coursed through her body, held her fast to where she now stood.

Is this the cloak I covered him with that day?

She held her breath and waited.

The man, now dressed in threadbare trousers and tunic shirt, was striding up the hill towards her, the horse alongside. All she seemed able to muster was a quaking hope that his intention was kind.

He cleared his throat, tossed curls off his forehead and asked: "Who are you, milady and what brings you here?"

Ah, a warm voice, a faint accent. . . He held his arms away from his body, hands open to show that he was unarmed and meant no harm. Yunitra faced him. The horse nudged the man's back as if to say: 'Come on get closer. She's a friend'. The man's intense gaze met her questioning eyes.

She found her voice.

"I'm Yunitra. Who are you and what are *you* doing here?"

While shyness threatened to overcome her curiosity she also felt a stirring liberation from the penance of silence and days and weeks of solitude.

She blushed.

He held her in his gaze, noticed the rosy flush in her cheeks.

Although only a few steps away from each other, they seemed intent on claiming the ground on which they stood. The air between them thrummed with a yearning to reach across what appeared to be an unbridgeable ravine.

"Uh, I'm Uwomo. I am here because this is where I halted my life as a fighter. And you, Yunitra?" He took a step towards her.

She took a step back but could not go further as the rock blocked her retreat.

"I am here because your horse — it is your horse isn't it? — brought me here."

Uwomo stroked the horse's velvety muzzle, "Yes, this is my faithful companion Maximus. The two of you don't appear to need a formal introduction to each other but I need to express our gratitude to you for re-uniting us."

Maximus stretched his neck to nuzzle Yunitra's ear just as she turned away from the man's smile, lost her balance and fell backwards onto the rock to land with a grunt as she was saying: "But why was he alone?"

"Uh, that's a long story Yunitra. . . but then I could ask the same of you, if I may: why are *you* here?"

"My story is a long one too; many beginnings. . . but, ummm I'm not sure of where I am."

I want to know this young woman sitting on my cloak. I want to run my fingers through those wild auburn curls crowning her head. And what's that shapeless sack she's covering her body with? Who would dress a beautiful young woman in such a thing? But then, how do I look in my tattered clothing? My cloak! That'll help. Maybe.

"I see that you're sitting on my cloak so, if you don't mind, Yunitra, I'd like to put it on."

"Oh, of course!" she blurted, to which he responded by extending his hand to her. Without thinking, she grasped his hand and rose from the rock to stand facing him. Her heart raced. Her hand tingled as if electrified by his firm grasp.

The dignity and courtesy he presented in that gesture closed the distance between them to a mere arm's length, brought a flush to her entire body and a tremulous desire to trust him. As he settled the cloak about his shoulders she glimpsed the scar on the side of his face. She remembered that scar. It had been a fresh wound when she had covered him with his cloak that day in the sunlit glade across the stream from her hilltop cave.

Shelter

Rain-filled clouds gathering on the horizon, roiled and churned. If Maximus had not become insistent with his nickering and hoof stamping neither Yunitra or Uwomo would have noticed the change in wind direction nor the chill it carried. When an icy drop of rain landed on Yunitra's cheek, she looked away from him and up at the darkening sky.

"We should find shelter or build something to keep us dry." she said, retrieving her sling bag to make certain it contained her tinder box. "Oh, and I'll collect kindling and a log or two. We need a fire."

Uwomo put on his boots, fastened the leather belt at his hips, sheathed the sword, put on the padded vest, replaced the cloak about his shoulders and went in search of shelter. Uwomo wondered about Yunitra: how long she might have been alone, about that flicker of recognition when she noticed the scar on his cheek, about how she and Maximus had bonded. He felt at a complete loss to understand any of it and resolved to take as long as necessary to find out.

He heard her call out, looked to where she stood some distance away, her arms loaded with kindling. "I've found a place. Bring some logs on your way back here."

Huh! She knows what she's doing, seems undaunted and yet. . . that endearing flush in her cheeks.

The shelter she had found was a deep hollow in the trunk of an ancient cedar tree. Traces of past travellers were evident near the mouth of the hollow: ashes and a partially burnt log in the centre of a ring of stones. The interior, though dark and smoke blackened, was clean. The ground encircling the massive trunk of the venerable old cedar was dry and fragrant. Yunitra liked the way the tree's lower branches created a canopy, felt certain Maximus would be sheltered and also well concealed.

Maximus – a most suitable name for a magnificent animal- he'll be safe and dry under those branches and this soldier, Uwomo and I will fit comfortably into the hollow. Comfortably? What am I thinking?

Rain was falling steadily by the time he came upon her kneeling at the ring of fire stones coaxing a slender flame. He placed, near her, logs he had kept dry under his cloak and then peered into the hollow.

"This is perfect; even high enough for me to stand up. Thank you, Yunitra. You're a resourceful woman. Where or, I should say, from whom did you learn these ways of survival?"

"Uh, we need food and fresh water . . . my bowl will catch rain but umm, do you know how to hunt?"

The word, 'hunt' hit Uwomo like a punch in the stomach. The order to hunt for mid-wives and healers; orders he had indiscriminately carried out and also the very real possibility that the order to hunt for him as a deserter would have already been set in motion. He looked away and did not respond to Yunitra's question. She noticed his jaw clenching, the sudden tightening in his shoulders, his fisted hands but it was the hollow dread in his eyes that prompted her to state: "Oh, I know what we can do about food. Here, you tend the fire while I forage for oysters and mussels. It won't take long and if I go right now before the daylight leaves, I'll return when the fire stones are hot enough to cook the food." This rush of words tumbled toward him while she grabbed her sling bag and turned to run to the sea shore. "Wait! Yunitra, wait! Take my cloak."

"No, it's too long, will slow me down."

"Well, put on my padded vest then. Please."

She stood still long enough to allow him to help her into the vest before she hurried down the hill away from him.

He watched her until she was a mere speck bent over a tidal pool. Rain dripping from his long hair into the neck of his tunic reminded him to tend the fire. Maximus, dry under sheltering branches raised his head from the pile of sweet hillside grass his master had cut for him to also watch Yunitra on the rocks.

Uwomo sat on his haunches warming his hands at a brightly burning fire, pondering over the mystery this young woman presented while silently pleading with Providence to guide and sustain him.

Her bowl, full to over-flowing, moved him to offer Maximus a drink. He replaced the empty bowl exactly where she had put it and felt a surge of pride in her ability to know these survival tasks. What had he learned about survival beyond the training to stay alive in battles and raids? Nothing, he thought to himself. So, how was he going to fulfill his dream of leading a gentle, sustainable life? The dream that had come to him after he had withdrawn his war sword. . . -oh, yes, the dream had included the tender caress of a loving woman but what was it he had asked the stars to reveal to him? Ah. The whereabouts of Maximus. That was it. And here, his horse had come to him. . . accompanied, no less, by a strong, practical woman.

Maximus whinnied to announce Yunitra's return and there she was, her curls flattened by rain, holding her fully laden sling bag out to him. Her slender bare arms looked as vulnerable as the legs of a new born butterfly emerging from a cocoon of his oversized vest hanging loosely about her slim body. He took the bag from her, amazed at the weight of it and realized how strong she actually must be to have carried it up the hill; effortlessly, it seemed.

"The oysters and mussels could be laid out on the stones now. Oh, here's your vest. Thanks. It kept me warm and dry but it does need a wash."

He took the vest from her, tossed it into the tree hollow thinking, *'if you only knew what that vest has witnessed you wouldn't want to be near me.'*

He squatted by the fire and withdrew the bounty: one closed shell at a time. She watched him marvelling at the efficient beauty of each oyster, each mussel and how, with a reverent bend of his head, he arranged the shells on hot stones. Although curious about his gnarled knuckles and his calloused palms it was the sensitivity in his long dextrous fingers that captured her, enthralled her into a momentary daydream.

Shells opened to release a mouth-watering aroma. Yunitra reached for one, prised it further open and offered Uwomo an intricately designed morsel of ocean flesh sitting in a pearly vessel. Repeating the process with an oyster for her self she cast him a glance of encouragement and tipped the flesh into her mouth. He sat motionless, an open oyster resting in the palm of one hand transfixed by her deliberation and wild grace.

"What are you waiting for, Uwomo?" Smacking her lips and wiping her chin with the back of her hand; "You must be hungry. Are you not accustomed to this food?"

"I'm . . . umm, eh, watching your deft manner of eating, Yunitra – I beg your pardon for staring. Yes, I am hungry." And he tilted back his head and slurped.

Empty shells mounted up into a tidy pile, another log was added to the fire as each of them silently contemplated the fall of night, the need to rest and the delicate balance between caution and mounting desire.

I suppose we'll both be sleeping in the hollow of this tree . . . lying next to each other. . . I'd like that but I'm . . . what? Afraid? He won't hurt me – will he? Damn this mistrust I feel!

"I'll bid Maximus a good night and return in moments. My padded vest could be a headrest and we could use my cloak to cover us"

Overcome with shyness mixed with traces of mistrust, she concentrated on folding the vest that she placed deep in the hollow. She was spreading out his cloak preparing to slide under it and to lie still with eyes closed when she sensed his presence at the entrance. He stood with feet apart, his hands busy with the unbuckling of his belt, the silhouette of him rimmed in light from a fire ring of embers.

She extended a hand to him saying: "Come, Uwomo."

He dropped sword and belt, removed his boots and came to where she knelt, her face glowing with tenderness turned up to him. He took her out-stretched hand in his and dropped to his knees inches from her. Until this moment he'd had no awareness of his height and breadth of shoulder in comparison to her light-boned slenderness and, afraid he might crush her bird-like frame he gently reached over her shoulder with his free arm drawing her to him. She wrapped her legs around his hips, nestled her face in the hollow of his throat, encircled his torso with her arms. The sheer force of her desire knocked him backwards onto his heels.

Her breath sent thrilling gusts of warmth across his chest, she nestled her face further into his neck to hear the steady beat of his pulse.

"I'm going to remove my clothes Yunitra."

"Hush. Nothing is more important than our safety, right now."

"But you'll have to let go of me for a moment. . . I need to stand up."

"Tear them off- I'll help."

"These are the only clothes I own and I'd like to keep them fairly intact. Please let go - just for a moment."

She would not let go of his hips and torso, so he did the next best thing: he stood up. Her legs slipped from his hips but her arms held on tightly, her feet dangled above the ground. He slid his hands into her armpits aiming to put her down safely when, with a squeal, she let go his torso and, her laughter ringing out like bells of celebration she toppled over onto the cloak. He untied his leggings stepped out of them and removed his shirt.

Nothing would halt his intention to hold her, caress her but her joyous laugh lifted his spirit into realms of unfettered delight. He fell down next to her, his laughter, unexpressed for so many years, bursting free.

Yunitra stroked scars on muscled shoulders, held his face, fingers traced the scar on his cheek and she found his mouth. Tentatively their lips met, the slurping of oysters momentarily flitting by.

"Oh, Uwomo. I like being close like this..." Her voice trailed off into a sigh as he stretched out on top of her, cradling her head in his linked arms. Their eyes met in an exchange of unspeakable wonderment. He inhaled the smell of her skin, her hair. Embers settled in the fire ring, sent sparks heavenward as night, drawing into the edges of the world occupied by Yunitra, Uwomo and Maximus, seemed to hesitate a moment at the outer tips of the cedar's branches as if to protect the three fugitives from harm before covering them and the dying fire in darkness.

Count Arrogar's Search

The Count, his two bodyguards and the four soldiers, having left the barracks fuelled with single-minded revenge some days ago, were now tired and disgruntled. They had combed the countryside for clues of the whereabouts of Uwomo and Maximus. They had searched one humble settlement after another, interrogated the inhabitants with no success whatsoever. As if the fruitlessness of their days was not enough to diminish determination, sleeping on hard ground had begun to take its toll on their loyalty to their task of finding Uwomo and Maximus. The Count, despite the comfort of his bed, quilts and pillows in his tent, was showing signs that his frail grip on reality was slipping.

To mask his frustration over what seemed to be a futile search, the Count feigned decisiveness by increasing his criticism of the men: abusing them verbally, spitting out his tea that he denounced as tasting of smoky horse piss, and grumbling about the food he declared only fit for animals. In his worst moments of despair, he threatened to castrate them for carelessness.

They all, including the Count, had become odorous: their boots, their armpits, their saddle-sore rear-ends and genitals. As much as the Count believed himself to be hardy and infinitely masculine, he was now forced to admit that he abhorred rough living.

And now, storm clouds building to the West robbed the late afternoon of sunlight and cast the fast-flowing river before them in a sinister light. Imminent rain forced them to halt and set up camp. No sooner had the bodyguards pitched and secured the Count's tent and seen to his needs, the storm wind roared through the forest. Twigs, leaves and river -sand carried by the gale struck the men, caused their retreat to shelter at the trunk of a willow and the horses to turn their backs to the onslaught. And then came the rain. It fell in sheets as if delivered by demons of hell and continued unabated for many hours, causing the river to rise in flood. The

Count's shouts to his bodyguards, drowned out by the roar of the storm remained unheard. The soldiers, resigned to the discomfort of drenched clothes and wet bedding, slept fitfully under the willow while the Count curled up in a foetal position under dry quilts, a pillow covering his head.

It was the utter silence that stirred them all to awake. Between over-hanging willow branches they could see traces of a rising sun. Drenched, cold, hungry and thoroughly fed up with this mission that appeared to have lost all purpose, they resorted to their soldierly discipline and went in search of wood for a fire.

Wet wood took time to catch alight. Tea-making was a slow process as was the cooking of flatbread from the mix that Cook had provided in their rations.

When the Count eventually emerged from his tent, the soldiers packed up ready to move on.

"Your Lordship, do we cross the river in order to continue the search for Uwomo and Maximus?"

"Why would you ask such a question? You fool!"

"The river has burst its banks, sir. It might be better to ride along this side sir, until a safer place is found to allow our passage across, your Lordship."

"Well, what are we waiting for, then? The day you develop a brain or a semblance of intelligence. . . Pah! Move on!"

The swollen river carrying branches and small trees roiled and heaved. The men eyed the bank as they rode in a westerly direction searching for a place where they could safely cross. At one such place where the river was wider and shallow, the soldier leading the group reined in his horse, raised his hand to signal a halt and shouted: "Your Lordship I see something that could be a clue. Your permission to inspect the item, sir?"

"May the devil take you if this is a ploy to slow us down! Go!"

The soldier dismounted, handed the reins to the rider behind him, and made his way down the muddy bank directly to a shiny object glinting in sand at the edge of the water. He gripped it in both hands, pulled it free and rinsed it. The Count leaned forward from his saddle: "What do you have there, soldier? Speak up!"

"This here is a shield, your Lordship."

"Well – bring it to me, damn you!"

The Count held the shield with trembling hands. Yes, this was the shield he clearly recalled handing to the young recruit, Uwomo, some years back. In a spasm of longing for his prize warrior, missing the comfort of his accommodation in the barracks, he teetered between wanting to dismiss the discovery of the shield as inconsequential in order to justify a return to barracks and, if he found Uwomo, at least he could derive some pleasure at beholding the beauty of the man one more time before killing him.

The soldiers turned their horses to face the Count who, masking his churning emotions stated:

"This is Uwomo's shield".

The group of seven riders - four soldiers facing the Count and his two bodyguards alongside – froze as if immobilized by the thought that Uwomo could be close by.

A bodyguard leaned towards the Count.

"We could continue along this side of the river until it reaches the ocean – shouldn't take us long, as the river itself, has become wider –an indication that it is getting closer to spilling into the sea. Sir?"

"Well, what are we waiting for?" The Count shouted. "Move along now. We'll continue the search on this side of the river."

He handed the shield to the bodyguard. "Stow this away in a safe place – your saddle bag will do."

Narrow Escape

The tree hollow had provided shelter from the night's storm and now Yunitra and Uwomo stirred from a deep untroubled sleep, disentangled their limbs from the close hold they had on each other. Forest birds awakened as fingers of sunlight reached through tree branches. A bright beam lingered at the entrance of the hollow tree, highlighting the pair on a rumpled cloak. Maximus could be heard moving about. And then he nickered.

Uwomo rose to his feet as if shot from a catapult. "That's a warning nicker, Yunitra. Collect our things, quickly. I'll take my sword and here, toss me my vest, please. Come!" Uwomo's urgency was contagious and Yunitra understood that they must flee. She packed her sling bag, grabbed the cloak, and stuffed that into her bag as well. Uwomo, his sword drawn and raised, moved with stealth and caution to Maximus. Yunitra joined him with a nudge to gain his attention. He turned to look at her. In that look she saw the warrior in the set of his jaw, the grip he had on his sword, the placement of his booted feet. But she also caught a glimpse of a resigned sorrow lurking around his eyes.

Uwomo put a finger to her lips to indicate silence then gestured toward Maximus and mimed that Yunitra mount the horse and that he, Uwomo, would lead them along the edge of the forest under cover of branches towards the ocean.

Uh -to the sea? But what do we do when we get there? Swim? Could this be harm coming our way? Uwomo seems. . . tense, not afraid but. . .

And she recalled his reaction to the word "hunt" when she had asked him if he knew how to do that. Yunitra's mind raced with fear of being pursued as Maximus turned his head to her indicating that he was ready for her to climb onto his back. But how was she going to do that? She stood for a moment eyeing the height of the horse and felt small and puny. Maximus lowered his head, his great mane fell towards her and she grabbed a fistful of the coarse luxuriant growth, heaved herself up onto his withers and wriggled backwards until she was astride his broad back.

Uwomo tried to conceal a smile of pride while indicating she lower her torso onto Maximus' neck. Then he stepped away from the tree trunk, took the tattered end of the tether rope that still hung about Maximus' neck. They made their way down the hill, along the edge of the forest, halting often to listen for pursuers.

"Yunitra" he whispered, "we will cross where the river flows into the bay – see the shallows there? And then make our way into those trees on the farther side. Do you see those rocks rising high, over there just beyond the trees? We will shelter within those. Keep moving!"

She peered through branches and could see exactly what he meant. *He's well-practiced . . . hmmm. . . I trust him! This feels good – as if our night in the tree hollow has something new added to it. . . here we are fleeing from danger and I'm no longer alone and afraid.* And with that realization, attraction suffused her entire body, pushed her to incline her face towards Uwomo for a kiss forgetting that she was on the back of Maximus. She tilted, lost her grip on the mane and began a slow slide off the horse's back. Uwomo, who was standing at Maximus' shoulder, his attention on their surroundings, sensed her closeness in time to halt her fall by catching her in the crook of his arm. "Oh, Uwomo! I'm sorry. My longing to kiss you overtook me. . . I forget where I am." She blushed.

"Yunitra, I don't think there's time to kiss – not right now. Can you wait until we're safely hidden?"

"You're right – yes, I understand but then let's hurry to safety so that we can, you know. . . um, kiss again."

Nodding his agreement, he hoisted her back up onto Maximus and they resumed their escape across the river's shallows, into the trees before making a dash for the columns of rock that resembled the walls and towers of a fortress. Here they entered a narrow passageway between sheer walls that, judging by the smell, was used by otters and seals. Now certain they were safely concealed, they both stood on Maximus' back at a cleft in the rock wall to watch the hill, the bay and the forest edge.

A Shield

The bodyguard took the shield from the Count, secured it in his copious saddlebag and at the Count's shout: "Move on!" the soldier at the head of the line kicked his horse into a steady walk.

They rode single file in silence. With renewed interest sparked by the discovery of the shield each man scanned the river bank on their right, the forest floor on their left. The discovery of the shield raised collective hope but, even so, each man also had his own sense of foreboding that ranged from dreading the outcome of finding Uwomo and his horse, the lengths to which the Count would exact punishment - which was dependent on his mood - and the extreme diligence required of them if the capture and return to barracks of their revered leader were to occur. Would they have to tie him with ropes to avert his escape? That possibility sickened each one of the soldiers.

The Count had momentary glimmers of a need to know what exactly it had been that caused Uwomo's disappearance but these glimmers became dim in comparison to his desire to inflict excruciating pain.

Late afternoon on that day the Count and his men emerged from the forest. Here the river flowed into a wide fan of shallow water rippling to meet the sea. To their left, the ground sloped up to the top of a hill where a flat-topped rock stood like an ancient seat. The lead soldier noticed that the grass around the rock appeared flattened as if trampled upon. Before them, a pebble beach, washed by waves that mingled with the river's flow. To their right, the bay curved away from where they had dismounted, to a distant point where towering rocks the height of a fortress appeared to guard that end of the bay.

The lead soldier, he who had found the shield, dismissed the gigantic rocks as impenetrable to any human and brought his searching eyes closer to the river's edge where a dislodged stone piqued his interest. He splashed through the shallows to inspect the stone and the place from where it had come loose. At the same time a second soldier made his way up the slope to investigate the trampled grass around the flat-top rock. The remaining two soldiers removed saddles and bridles from all the horses, tethered them upstream to graze and drink and set up camp. The bodyguards pitched the Count's tent under the sheltering branches at the forest's edge. Once the soldiers had a fire going, they began to prepare a meal for His Lordship and themselves.

A sense of order prevailed: food was cooking, clothes and bedding were drying, horses were resting and the Count was comfortably seated on a cushion on a log, his feet warming at the fire. Both hands cupped the edge of the shield that lay on his lap,

The first soldier returned from inspecting the dislodged stone and the area surrounding it. He could not be certain of whether the previous night's rainstorm had simply washed it loose or if some passer-by had knocked it. He was, however, reluctant to draw any conclusion because he had begun to think that Uwomo was best left alone to carry out his escape.

The Count looked up from contemplating the shield and, to hide the wistfulness he had drifted into, he scratched at his chin and barked out at the soldier:

"Well, soldier – speak up! What did you find?"

"Nothing of interest, your Lordship."

"Very well. We will await a verdict from that one." The Count wagged his fingers towards the soldier returning from his investigation of the area around the flat-topped rock on the hillside.

"Do you have something to report or, like him, have you also somehow, found nothing of interest? What was up there on the hillside? Speak up, idiot! If you lot have brought me here – yes here, to this dead end for nothing, I'll see you all whipped!"

"Your Lordship there are marks of human activity but last night's rain has washed away footprints. Eh, and hoof prints if there were ever any there."

"Oh, curse this mission! Uwomo be damned to rot in hell and your horse with you!" And the Count flung the shield into the blazing fire.

Soldiers and bodyguards stood open mouthed staring at the shield as flames licked away its legendary gleam, blackening it beyond recognition.

"Get away from me! Get to work. . ." The Count coughed and waved his arms as if to dispel smoke from the fire- "Stop staring!"

Towers Of Rock

Uwomo and Yunitra, standing on Maximus' back observed the Count and his men who were some distance away but clearly visible in the light of the fire and the slanted rays of a setting sun. The Count's gestures, whether in repose as he gazed at something on his lap or speaking to the soldier on his return from the flat-top rock showed an uncontrolled parody of being in charge; gestures all too familiar to Uwomo.

What a bedraggled group of men they are! Milling about like lost boys and as for that Count and his slaves – pah! Bodyguards indeed!

Hearing Uwomo's grunt, Yunitra turned from peering through the cleft to see his face twist with disgust.

"Uwomo, who are those people?"

"They are searching for me and for Maximus,"

"Why would they do that? Uwomo, please tell me."

"Yunitra I do want to tell you – uh, I don't know where to begin. . ." Maximus shifted under the weight of the pair standing on his back as if to tell his fellow fighter to speak his story. Uwomo climbed down fully expecting to begin his self-revealing account to Yunitra.

"Here, come down" he said extending his hand up to her. Yunitra, with no idea of how to gracefully descend from the back of a war- horse held onto Uwomo's hand and slid down over the barrel-sized ribs of Maximus into Uwomo's arms. But, instead of embracing her, he put his hands on her shoulders, rested his forehead on her head.

"We need to find food, Yunitra – for Maximus and ourselves – any ideas?"

"Yes, I do have some ideas but let's wait until that group around the fire are asleep".

A short while later when the soldiers had bedded down for the night and their horses were hobbled under trees and before she went foraging for food, Yunitra wanted to know who that was in a tent lit from within.

Once she was settled next to him he began his telling of how he had met Count Arrogar.

"You see, Yunitra, at the time I was working with Grandfather in his blacksmith workshop, the search for recruits to join the army fighting to uphold the new law was under way. Do you know about the new law?" Yunitra nodded and shivered. "Well, that beast of a man, who is in that tent right now, brought to Grandfather's workshop, countless weapons and shields, armor too, that needed repair. . . that's when I met him. That's when I agreed to select a sword – this sword I carry - from the repaired weapons – curse my youthful pride! That's when that man ordered me to report to the barracks. . .if I had disobeyed his order he would have destroyed the lives of my family."

"Hush, Uwomo – we don't want them to hear us – hush now. You saved the lives of your family and you're alive! That's good – isn't it?"

With her hand on his cheek, she entreated him to look into her eyes. His heart lurched at the infinite depth of her earnest blue-eyed gaze.

Arrgh! This is one of the hardest things I've yet encountered in my life: acceptance of her presence as a shared support, the "we" of us as a twosome of humans. All I've known since my time with grandfather is my trust of Maximus.

But then the more pressing and immediate need for food arose again. In the same instant, as if she had heard his thought, Yunitra lifted her sling bag onto her shoulder, crept away from their hiding place, scanned the surroundings, found that all was quiet and waving her fingers, she sprinted away towards the forest.

He watched her disappear like a wraith into the dark trees with an ache in his heart at the missing of her. He drew close to Maximus "My friend and trusted steed help me understand. Stand by me and let us ask the night spirits to return her safely to us." Maximus turned and nuzzled Uwomo's neck and blew a gentle snort into his hair.

Yunitra passed the four soldiers asleep near a dying fire, continued towards the Count's tent where two men lay like logs at its entrance. Although unmoving, the impression of guarding reminded her to move with stealth and speed. She skirted the horses hobbled under the trees, gathered roots and tubers in a bank that had become exposed by the rain-swollen river, stuffed these into her sling bag then doubled back towards the tower of rocks. On her way she stopped to pick late summer berries and to wrench an armload of grasses from the ground. Then she crouched down at the edge of the trees to prepare for a swift dash across open ground. The sleeping soldiers had not stirred and nothing had changed at the Count's tent.

We need water — fresh water. Dare I approach the edge of the shallows? Oh, but I won't be able to run with a bowl of water and it's imperative I run from here, across that sand, then the pebbles and into our hiding place as swiftly as my feet will carry me. By the look on Uwomo's face, those men mean to capture him and Maximus too. Pay attention — get ready now. . .

She sped across open ground and slipped into the passageway.

Uwomo's relief at seeing her spurred him forwards with his arms open to receive her, to hold her. She slipped the sling bag from her shoulder, dropped the bundle of grass and leaned into the strong warmth of his body.

A sliver of moon rising over the forest cast a pearly glow on waves lapping to meet the river. Yunitra and Uwomo, covered by the cape, leaned against the rock wall chewing on raw tubers. The wild earthy food took her mind back to the cave, and a sudden longing for the fire, the ring of hot stones and how much better tubers tasted when cooked to a warm softness.

"These taste very good when cooked. . . but, no matter, they can sustain us for a while". Uwomo could no longer hold back his curiosity: "You've eaten these things before, Yunitra?" "Yes, Uwomo, I have. I would make a fire in a ring of stones. . . and then. . . ". Uwomo hung on every word as she described, in loving detail, the cave, the stream, the birds, her daily rituals.

Not all of it though. Somehow she felt a need to withhold her discovery of him and Maximus in that forest glade, how an instinctual urge to tend to him had overcome her fear, had led her to cover his supine body with his cape. Also, she withheld recounting the day following when she had found the glade empty, the day her innocence broke under the weight of an inexplicable desire. Those two days she kept safely tucked away in her heart.

The Count's Nightmare

The Count could not sleep. He felt claustrophobic in his tent; heard rustling in an otherwise silent night in the forest. His heart pounded and a bitter taste of defeat coated his tongue. He struggled to reach full consciousness while angrily kicking at his bedding, fighting the terrifying images in his mind of flames licking at his ankles, his entire battalion turning into a sea of open-mouthed faces mocking him.

He called to his bodyguards who came to him immediately. They lit a lamp pretending to have not noticed the disarray of quilts and pillows, not to have caught the stench of sweat.

"How much longer before daybreak?"

"Judging by the moon, Sir, I'd say about three hours."

"Curse this night! Bring me a flagon of wine."

One bodyguard reached into a satchel that contained the Count's personal effects, extracted a flagon of wine and a silver cup that he placed on the Count's bedside table.

"Well, pour it, damn you!

The Count drank hungrily in continuous swallows until the cup was empty

"Pour again and bring me the slop bucket."

The Count relieved himself into the bucket.

"Empty that," indicating the bucket, "then leave me."

Maximus snorted. Uwomo 's mind, filled with imagining Yunitra living in a cave, picturing her bathing in the stream, returned reluctantly to the present moment. They climbed onto the back of the horse to peer through their now familiar observation place. From there they saw the Count's tent glowing with light two big bodies moving slowly from one side of the tent to the other.

"What's that about, Uwomo?"

"The Count is not comfortable and needs help from his loyal guards. That's what could be going on. . . "

"But. . . oh, I don't know, Uwomo – what's the matter with him?"

"My estimation of him is colored by . . . what would you call it? Distrust? Disgust maybe? Uh, it could be that his demons are getting the better of him. He's a sick man. But, Yunitra, for now let us be quiet and watchful. Neither you, nor Maximus nor I need that man to discover us. Believe me, please."

When the tent had become dark once again, Yunitra in a whisper, asked Uwomo why the Count would be searching for him just as a realization struck her: that he, this gentle loving man sitting close by her side; this tantalizingly warm and courteous man had been trained to kill. She shuddered at the thought of how immensely difficult it must have been for him to do that: to kill. "But I still don't understand. You reported to the barracks, you trained as a soldier. . . you did as you were ordered to do… so, why are they searching – actually, it seems that they are hunting for you! Oh, Uwomo! What did you do to warrant this?" She reached for his face and placed her hand over the scar on his cheek. "I need to know, Uwomo."

Ah, her small warm hand on my cheek, that smudge of earth on her resolute chin – oh, heaven! Please let her strength support her, let her not judge me as a coward. I could not bear that.

Uwomo cupped her chin, held her gaze with his own deep dark eyes and answered. "I am a deserter."

"You must have had a good reason to do that, Uwomo. I can't imagine what that reason could be but. . . Tell me, please."

He had expected her to withdraw her hand from his cheek, to recoil from him in shock or dismay and when none of this occurred, he slowly let out the breath he had been holding. She then turned from sitting next to him to straddle his lap to be face to face. "Tell me, Uwomo, what spurred you to desert? We have the rest of the night before it becomes necessary to spy on that group hunting for you."

"Yunitra, have you ever felt the loss of empathy for your fellow humans?"

"Uh hu - I've felt a lack of empathy *from* others – my parents for instance, my mother actually. Why do you ask?"

"From the day I reported to Count Arrogar at the training ground, I had to put behind me all that was dear to me. The only way I knew how to shut away the loss of a life I'd dreamed about living – as a blacksmith - was to discipline myself to feel nothing. . . well, as little as possible. Maximus saved me from becoming an unfeeling monster of a man."

"But how were you able to kill, Uwomo? What was in your mind when you did that – killed a person?"

"Oh, Yunitra that's the source of my self loathing! I don't remember feeling. . . I drew the heat of attack into my core and let my physical power carry out the act. Since the day I deserted I've been struggling to recall times and moments that might show me that a sense of decency remains within me - even a mere shred."

"Part of my story, Uwomo, that I haven't told you, yet, is about the moment I had to decide between fulfilling my duties which would have placed me in danger and of fleeing from danger which meant turning my back on duties for which I was responsible . . . Was that what drove you to desert?"

"um. . . not quite. Remember my asking you about empathy – if you'd ever lost it? I realized how deadened I'd become to the suffering of others when – just in time, I believe – I recognized the village I was preparing to raid -it was the place I'd been born- uh, the village where my parents and Grandfather lived. . . by obeying the order to be recruited I'd believed that I was saving my family from punishment but then there, I found myself poised to punish them! I had to turn away, had to leave. . . had to desert the army if I had any hope of finding my human-ness."

"Oh, Uwomo – we're both fugitives! At least you are missed by those who know you, whereas I don't think anyone would remember me."

Return To Barracks

The absence from barracks of the Count, his bodyguards and four soldiers had little affect on Cook's daily provision of food to the army. He was not missing the added duty of preparing fine meals for the Count, though, and had to admit to enjoying the lack of pressure and fastidious demands placed on him to keep the Count satisfied. He was thinking about this when a young boy ran into the kitchen, shouting: "Cook! Oh, master Cook I carry a message – his lordship will be here by sundown, expects his quarters to be prepared for his return – uh. . ." The boy raised his hand and counted, finger by finger: "Fresh bedding, flagons of wine, hot water to bathe in, poached fish and sweets with Cognac."

"A well-carried message young pup. Fleet-footed too. Hmmm? Seems to me you could do with a bowl of soup before your return home. Here, bring me a bowl from that stack over there." Cook ladled a good chunk of meat into the bowl, added broth and vegetables and a chunk of bread.

"I thank you, master cook" and being too small to reach the table, the boy sat down to eat on the stone floor near to the massive hearth.

Cook turned his broad back to the boy and feigned an interest in the loaves of bread cooling on a window sill. He was disturbed by the news of the Count's return not only because his reprieve from the Count's demands was to come to an end but, if he were to be honest, he had held an unspoken hope that Uwomo and Maximus had not been captured. *Surely they could not have been discovered in such a short time: fewer days than the fingers on both my hands! But then, perhaps Uwomo gave himself up? Nah! I don't think so. So, what then, took place out there?*

The soldier leading the returning search party, reined in his horse at the crest of a hill from where the buildings that comprised the barracks were visible. While he waited for the Count, the bodyguards and the other three soldiers to come abreast, he took in the familiar configuration of wood and stone structures: the dormitories that formed a square within which stood the drill grounds and, adjacent to those, the low building that held the kitchen and eating hall not far from the stables. Smoke rising from the chimney of the Count's quarters that were set back from the barracks behind a high hedge indicated that the message of their return had reached Cook in good time. Relieved, he turned in his saddle to gauge the distance between himself and the approach of the Count and the search party. The group's progress had slowed to a halt, the Count's agitated gestures showed panic and anger. The bodyguards' horses strained at the bit while the three rearguard soldiers seemed to be waiting for instructions.

Eventually, the group moved towards him but the Count, instead of riding at the head of the line, rode at the tail end.

"His Lordship", a soldier informed him," has ordered us to proceed ahead of him. Lead on then, and hurry up! Cook will have received a message about our return and will surely have a good meal and ale ready for us."

At the sound of horses clattering into the stable-yard, every man seated at table with a bowl of soup, bread and ale at hand, looked up wide-eyed and nervous. Cook turned from the hearth and stood as still as the trunk of a tree, ladle in hand.

The four returning soldiers entered the hall, proceeded to the stack of bowls, took one each, walked to where Cook was standing and held out their bowls to be served.

As he ladled soup, Cook put his question to the soldiers by raising his eyebrows. The answer he received from them was an imperceptible shake of the head. Cook maintained an implacable expression on his broad sweaty face to hide the immense relief he felt.

No Uwomo or Maximus! Hail Heaven and all the stars above! How can this be – eh? I plan to find out as soon as this lot is fed, I will take the Count's meal to his quarters myself. I have to know – I'll sleep better knowing that Uwomo is free.

Cook did indeed sleep well. The Count, however, did not. Despite bathing in hot scented water, despite the soft silk robe he was wearing, despite an excellent and most welcome meal – the fish was flavoured to perfection - despite plenty of wine, the Count remained dispirited and deeply shaken over his failure to capture Uwomo and Maximus.

By morning, he had decided against speaking the honest truth about the fruitless search and had, instead, devised a cunning angle to his account of it. He dressed with care and summoned his bodyguards.

The entire battalion stood at attention in the cold morning air, their eyes riveted to the empty throne-like chair on the raised platform.

Count Arrogar stepped up onto the platform, marched to the chair, but, rather than sitting, he stood in front of it: "You! Men! Soldiers of the new law! Hear me now! Heed what I say." In the stillness of the morning the Count's voice, reedy and high-pitched, echoed off the walls of the buildings surrounding the drill grounds. "Without my diligent training Uwomo would not have become the great and fearless warrior you know and revere. It was due to my tireless attention and guidance that he became the warrior he is."

Cook, who was standing in a corner near the kitchen entrance, cleared his throat and spat onto the ground. "My arse! Your attention to Uwomo was fuelled by adoration of the young man." He muttered this in a hoarse whisper, covering his mouth to be sure he was not heard.

The Count, buoyed by the sound of his own voice extolling his personal success, continued: "It is to me that Uwomo owes his prowess. But, it is also the reason he escaped capture."

A sigh of relief rippled through the amassed soldiers. That collective exhalation of breath enveloped the Count with dread, crumbled his shaky resolve. He stumbled backwards to sit and continued: "Is Uwomo a man of honor? No, he is not. He deserted his post as a soldier, turned his back on you all and to his sworn allegiance to uphold the new law. If he is courageous enough to return to barracks of his own volition, I will consider holding him prisoner for his life-time and not put him and Maximus to death. But if he. . ." The Count lost his train of thought as the image of Uwomo's shield, licked by flames, blackened in a fire. The threat he was about to voice to the waiting audience died on his lips.

The amassed men stared at their boots in silence. Expecting a resounding cheer and hearing none, the Count became visibly unnerved; his hands trembled, his voice cracked as he ordered the men to dismiss. Then his bodyguards stepped forward to assist the Count who was struggling to rise from the throne-like seat. They escorted him away from the platform.

Part Two

Arrival Feast

Burning logs settle with a crackle, send sparks flying into an evening sky. At shore-line people prepare salmon to cook over the fire. Others arrange heaps of wild berries in a wood feast bowl. Evergreen trees near to Uwomo and Yunitra's dwelling on the low rise behind the gathered throng, release a heady scent that mixes with smoke from the fire. A receding tide bares rocks from which a bounty of oysters and mussels will soon be picked and arranged on hot stones at the fire's edge.

Seated on a grass mat, a baby boy at her breast, Yunitra gazes at the vast expanse of ocean – serene and benign this evening – and shudders with the memory of being captured by its unremitting power. But then, she reminds herself, it was that powerful wave that had brought her here into the warmth and life-giving generosity of this island and its people.

Uwomo, never too far from her side, stands tall and straight-backed taking in the tranquil scene of a community preparing food for a feast. Between Yunitra and Uwomo, their three- year-old daughter, Veritas, rests her head of ink-black curls on her mother's thigh. Maximus, ever the loyal guard, a few paces away from his human family, raises his head to catch the sea breeze blowing through his mane and forelock.

The island community are gathered to celebrate the anniversary of the arrival of Uwomo, Yunitra and Maximus three summers past. "Arrival" is how this day was named by the island Elders after a towering wave – more like a wall of ocean water – had deposited first Yunitra, then Uwomo , followed by Maximus, on the shore of this island.

As honoured guests of the "Arrival" celebration, it is only fitting, insist the islanders, that the couple, their offspring and their loyal horse be served rather than the island custom of helping one's self from the communal table.

Veritas on the mat next to her mother is served a plate-sized clam shell filled with pieces of her favourite food. Uwomo accepts a laden plank that he will share with Yunitra. Their baby boy, Exacta, now sleeps soundly on the mat between them. Maximus is served a bundle of sweet grass.

Starlight brightens as the sun slips down at an ink-blue line on the horizon. More logs are added to the fire.

In a voice as resonant as the log drum she strikes, Elder Wise Woman's words reach far beyond the community at the fire.

"One thousand days ago Our Mother Ocean rose up into a wall of water so powerful that we believed her mighty waves would swallow us all. If our friend, Albatross, had not warned us of the coming of the wave, we would indeed have perished. We fled to the summit of our highest mountain. We huddled together to watch Mother Ocean unleash her power onto our island. She took away trees, houses, canoes. . . but she took not one of us. Instead, Mother Ocean delivered a gift to us; a gift of two humans – a woman and a man - and one animal, a horse. We now come together to celebrate the gift of their arrival, to hear their story and to raise our spirit of gratitude."

In response to her open-palmed gesture towards Uwomo, Yunitra and Maximus, everyone calls out assent: "O-hu zuhto".

Uwomo lifts Veritas onto his shoulders, reaches for Yunitra who now has Exacta safely tucked into a cloth sling over her shoulder and they rise together. Maximus approaches to stand behind his loved humans.

Uwomo speaks.

"Far far away Mother Ocean washes the shores of a different land; a land where soldiers hunt and kill healers who are women; a land where I had served as a soldier until I deserted. A land where soldiers hunted for me with the intention of killing me and Maximus. The gods of Providence introduced Yunitra to me and to Maximus when she, also, was fleeing from soldiers. A search party looking for Maximus and me came very close to finding the three of us but we eluded capture by hiding in a passageway between walls of stone at the ocean's edge. The soldiers and their leader must have given up on their search for us because they departed early one morning. Not long after they had gone away we heard a sound we did not recognize – a sound so huge and deep it could have been the opening of the gates to Hades. . . then the earth trembled and a hissing grew into a loud sucking sound. We ran from our place of hiding to be struck by a fierce gale and to witness the retreat of the ocean. In those moments of complete incomprehension Mother Ocean returned as a wall of water. She roared and rose higher and higher until the sky was no longer visible. Then she swallowed us."

Yunitra picks up their story.

"When I surfaced, Mother Ocean was calm although heaving in swells as if her breathing were labouring after exerting a mighty energy. There was no sign of Uwomo, no sign of Maximus and no land in sight. Floating trees rose and fell with the swells. I took hold of the trunk of a young tree and wrapped my arms and legs around it. Thus the tree and I kept company under a dark storm-filled sky on the heaving breast of Mother Ocean. I must have slept or maybe lost consciousness; for how long I cannot say but if the dolphins could tell me, we might know. A school of them, squeaking and whistling, some leaping from the water in graceful arcs, others swimming under my body brought me to shore -this shore where we are now gathered."

"And my friend and me ", piped up the voice of a lean wild-haired boy, "we found her!"

"Yes, you did find me Lundi. And what was the first thing you did for me?"

"My friend Mano poured sweet water onto your lips and sat with you while I ran very fast to tell Elder Wise Woman to come. I was right in thinking Elder Wise Woman would know what to do."

"My old legs, they do not move swiftly anymore so I asked Lundi, here" and the old woman placed her hand lovingly on Lundi's head, "to run to Old Man Thunder with the message that he was needed at the shore. I collected my medicine bag and came down to the shore where I found Mano and this woman, whom you now know as Yunitra. She was lying on her side, her arms locked around the trunk of a tree. I called to her. She did not move. I knelt by her, stroked her hair away from her face, applied salve to her cracked lips, noticed the rise and fall of her chest. She was alive. But how was I to prise her arms away from the tree? I called to the spirits of the healing world to give me a sign. They responded instantly:

"With the shaft of a gull feather trace a direct path from the crown of her head to the base of her spine and then return on that path of her spine up to her crown with the soft end of the feather." That's what I did – twice – and on the third try she arched her back away from the tree which freed one arm – so limp, almost life-less.... ah, but she was breathing. I wanted to get her into a sitting position but her other arm was trapped by the weight of the tree trunk. Mano, who had watched every step of my ministrations, noticed my puzzlement and offered a most clever suggestion: to free her other arm he would dig away the sand to make space under the tree trunk and then slide out her arm. He immediately set himself to the task of digging and so, when Lundi and Old Man Thunder came upon us they found Yunitra sitting, covered with my shawl and sipping water. Before I covered her near naked body with my shawl, though, I had noticed she was clearly with child – early in the cycle. Yes, our playmates, the dolphins, brought us two gifts in one that day. We will thank them when they visit at moonrise tonight."

Uwomo places a hand on Yunitra's shoulder, she moves close enough to rest her cheek on his chest as he speaks of the next part of his "Arrival" story.

"No battle I ever fought had overpowered me as did the force of Mother Ocean on that day. She pulled me down, down into a cauldron of churning sand, seaweed and debris. I fought to hold my breath and asked Mother Ocean to release her hold on me. I wondered if there was a sea creature who could carry me to the surface; a creature like those described to me by Grandfather in my childhood. In the guttering light of candles burning low his gestures cast enormous shadows on the lime-washed walls; shapes that brought to life tales of monster-like animals that lived in oceans. My struggle to free my self from Mother Ocean's hold on me weakened and with what I believed would be my last breath I called out to Grandfather and surrendered to the deep dark water. I still fail to find words to describe what took place following my surrender. So, as I do each year, I ask that you imagine with me this experience: a great force plucked me from the brink of death, threw me high above the water into light. Air rushed into my starved lungs. As my body fell towards the waves a giant of a sea creature, whom I now know to be Whale, surfaced in time to stop my fall by offering her back for me to land on. Thus she brought me to shallow water where I slid off her back. In so doing I looked into her eye and found there, knowledge and wisdom so filled with compassion and the power of all life, that I vowed to live in gratitude and kindness to my dying day."

Embers in the bonfire settle into a bright dome of heat. People shift from the perimeter to gather closer to the fire. In the East a full moon begins her rise into a sky carpeted with stars, the ocean erupts with dolphins dancing over the waves to the greeting calls of all present.

"And what of Maximus?" Uwomo continues. "If our loyal and staunch companion could use words I wonder what he would tell us about his arrival on this island?" Hearing his name, Maximus nuzzles Uwomo's neck, blows puffs of air into Yunitra's hair. Veritas giggles and asks to be lifted from her father's shoulders onto the broad back of Maximus. Exacta, snug in the sling over his mother's belly, stirs and stretches with a wide yawn. Three generations of islanders settle into warm sand, their bellies full and their minds listening as one.

"Perhaps a shoal surrounded him and guided him to shore? We know that it was the time of mating in the world of herring when shoals are present in abundant quantity. The other thing we know is, that the children. . ." Here Uwomo extends both hands in the direction of the island children sitting close together, "heard a strange calling sound coming from the grove of birch trees. Yes, children, your curiosity led you to investigate and it was there in the trees you came upon a giant smoke-grey creature with four legs, hair flowing from its neck and tail. I met some of you running from the grove in search of an adult. We hurried to where you'd discovered this creature, all talking at once, I understood it was the loneliness in the creature's call that touched your hearts; not a fear of a large unknown creature but the sound of its voice. Not one of us will forget that moment when the "creature", our Maximus, saw me, how, neighing loudly, he trotted in an urgent gait directly to me. I put my arms about his neck and it was then I found seaweed and many tiny silver fish tangled in his mane and forelock. You, children, instantly recognized the fish as herring. Thank you for trusting that he too was part of the "gift", otherwise his stout heart may have despaired once again."

Old Man Thunder clears his throat rises, grasps a hold of his medicine staff - an intricately carved tree branch, the thickness of a man's arm that is crowned with a rosette of feathers held in place by a bracelet of abalone shells.

"We Elders have lived long enough to remember despair. This is not a life-giving state for any one. Our despair arose in us when we were hunted by people who took our land from us and forced us into slavery. Their ways were cruel and disrespectful of life. We fled in the night on rafts, some in leaky canoes. Many drowned but those of us you see today were carried to safety by Mother Ocean. We made a vow then that our future generations would not be treated in any way that would cause despair. And that is one of the agreements this community lives by. So, Uwomo and Yunitra, and you, Maximus will not know despair again. Above all, your children will continue to live in a world of life-giving generosity, respect and care."

Old Man Thunder raises his medicine staff, his voice resonant with passion and power, calls to all gathered to join him in the invocation:

"O- hu zhuto!"

Their united voices reach the dolphins at the breakwater. Squeaking and whistling, their gleaming bodies leap in and out of a path of light laid out before them by Sister Moon on the breast of Mother Ocean sparkling under a blanket of stars.

Manona

Uwomo's mother, Manona, thinks of him every day. His presence seems to almost materialize when she visits the graves of her husband who was killed in the raid and her aged father the blacksmith. The first time this sensing of Uwomo occurred, Manona felt paralyzed by conflicting emotions of fear and hope: fear that he had been found by Count Arrogar which could mean he was suffering punishment, hope that he was free and thriving wherever he had escaped to.

Recently, her daily visits to the graves have taken on a subtle change in her experience of being at the burial site. She now looks forward to visiting the graves and to receiving this sensation of her son's nearness. *He feels alive and vigorous so it's not a 'ghost', not an 'apparition' – no - he would have to have died to be either of those – surely?*

Thus, in her mind, she has named 'it' a presence. Furthermore, to protect herself from being labeled a witch, she guards her secret with utmost care. Some of her village neighbours, observing her lightness of step on her return from the graveyard have grown suspicious of Manona's apparent happiness. Some women, embittered by their past misfortune whisper behind hands held over their mouths. "After all the hardship and loss we have endured at the hands of Count Arrogar and his soldiers, how could she be happy? Something is afoot, I tell you." Manona, fully aware of the gossip is not interested in allaying their assumptions or explaining her deeply felt reunion with her son – however immaterial he seems. And so, she continues to carry out her chores and to provide support to those who need her help. The gossip peters out as one by one the women come to the conclusion that Manona finds solace at the graves in the spirit of her father and also that of her husband.

Then, on a day that seems to be like any other, life in the village suddenly changes. The goat herder, Darr and his grand daughter, Macushla are sitting in the shade of a hawthorn tree - the goats not far from them - when Macushla sees a lone rider rein in his horse on the crest of the hill on the road that leads into the village square.

She nudges her grandfather: "Darr – look! There at the top of that hill – look! It's a man on a horse. Can your old eyes see him?" "Dimly, Macushla – but he seems to have come to a halt. Why is that, I wonder. He could not be a scout, could he? – one of that despicable Count's men – could he?" "Darr, we have not been plagued by any soldiers for many seasons. Remember the talk at market in town about Count Arrogar? He is ill, we are told, and was taken away. The barracks are deserted. It was Cook who spread the news. Do you recall his words, Darr?"

"Ah, Macushla, memories of the invasion, the people we lost to the swords, the village in ruins. . . those memories are as clear as if it had happened yesterday but our recent day at market seems lost to me now. Well, if that rider is not a scout who could it be?"

The rider kicks his horse into a trot and continues down the hill to eventually enter the village square. Others have also seen the rider, still others hear the clatter of the horse's hooves on the cobblestones. Contrary to a collective fear of unknown riders entering their village, curiosity spurs people to run to the square; each praying to the heavens, Manona among them.

Darr and Macushla hurriedly pen the animals and enter the square to the unmistakeable resonance of Manona's voice calling out to the rider: "Stay where you are and state your business!"

The rider responds: "I am a son of this village that I called home before Count Arrogar. . ." he spits onto the ground, "forced me into soldiery." People draw nearer. Macushla, takes hold of Darr by the arm and steers him closer to the rider. "Darr, you know that voice, Darr – listen! If I'm not mistaken that's my brother. Oh, Darr speak to him, please."

"Young man, tell us more of who you are. My failing eyes see very little but your voice carries some . . ."

"I am Darum, grandfather. She who stands with you is my sister, Macushla. I beg to be permitted to dismount."

Cries and shouts of joyous welcome rise from all gathered there. Macushla supports Darr as he stumbles towards his grandson who catches the old man against his chest to encircle him with both arms. One hand reaches for his little sister thus bringing her to stand at grandfather's back enabling Darum to embrace them both at once. In the melee of welcoming greetings, someone leads the horse to the drinking trough and another unties the saddlebags that they then place in grandfather's doorway.

As night draws into the valley people congregate around a bonfire in the square to hear Darum tell his story of how it was that he was home: home to stay.

While he waits for people to gather, as his grandfather had instructed him to do, he has time to look into their faces now illuminated by fire light. *I've known these people all my life and yet some are hard to recognize – perhaps they're not as I remember them in my young mind back then. . . how long was I away? Close to seven years? . . . lines in their faces, furrowed brows seem to have deepened. I sense a pall of. . . pain. Of course! Those absent from the fire must have perished. Oh my heaven - they are grieving.*

People settle on benches, others on milking stools, many on reed mats spread on the cobblestones. Darum stands next to his grandfather who is seated in a chair with Macushla at his feet.

Manona claps her hands and calls out a greeting that instantly quietens chatter and knits the people into a gathering focussed on the reason they are all there: to hear Darum's story and the news he carries.

Some years have passed since the entire village had come together in the square; a time many were not likely to forget as much as they tried. That was the day their homes, their livelihoods and many loved ones had perished under the flaming torches and slashing swords of the soldiers. That was also the day Manona had heard the name of her son spoken by one of the soldiers.

Over time memories of violent and unjust treatment and the overwhelming sense of loss have eased. Not the least of it attributable to the tenacious drive of villagers to assist each other with rebuilding their homes that served to lift the spirit of hope in those who had been close to giving up on life altogether. And now, here is Darr's grandson, recruited years ago, standing in their midst and ready to begin his story.

"My hand on grandfather's shoulder is helping me accept that I am truly here rather than in a dream I have held since I saw you last. Words to show you my gratitude for being alive and home with you, fail me. I'm not certain of what kind of man I have become and it is my fervent hope that whomever I am now will be accepted by you". An elderly woman cries out: "You are one of ours and whatever ails you will be cured by us, here in your home village." "That is my hope and I thank you for believing in me. But, as I have felt the cold hiss of death at my back, so have I also caused many deaths of innocent people. I struggled with the demons hounding me; fought against senseless murder until just a scant few weeks ago when I noticed the number of soldiers and their horses dwindling like a stream drying up in drought. Orders to carry out raids were few and far between. What was happening? We asked each other but nobody seemed to know until we asked Cook who told us this:

The Count, struck down by an illness, was ordered by the priest of the parish to recuperate at the coast, far distant from these parts. The priest believed the Count's illness was due to the devil's work and could be contagious. Count Arrogar upon arriving at the coast, in the company of his bodyguards, immediately set sail in a ship bound for other lands. Since, no leader has taken the Count's place and the raiding and killing frenzy has died down. Cook suggested we eat well, feed our horses and leave the 'hellhole'- that's what Cook called the barracks – a 'hellhole' - within the week, as he too, would be packing up to return to his home town."

Here Darum pauses in the telling of his news to absorb the rapt and loving attention of his friends and family. Someone begins to sing a song that has been forbidden by the authorities for years. Tentative voices join in, grow stronger, more adamant until the square thunders with the collective power of voices releasing fear and finding hope.

Manona makes her way around the periphery of the circle of people towards Darum. Her need to speak to him about Uwomo, although acute, does not blind her to the cohesion inspired by the liberating force of the song. She waits while some wipe tears, others turn to hold each other and yet others gather up their young to return to their homes. The fire has died down to a bed of embers. Darum senses her presence behind him and turns to speak to her.

"Manona, mother of Uwomo, greetings to you."

"Darum, son of our village, greetings to you. I hold a question that is burning my mind. Do you have news of Uwomo?"

"Ah, Uwomo. . . how long since you had news of your son?"

"Too long, Darum – uh, the day four soldiers razed our village to the ground, I overheard one of them saying my son's name. . . but nothing since that fateful day."

"Your son's name was on everyone's lips every day – more so in the eating hall at the barracks. We, the soldiers, revered him, longed to be chosen to accompany him on raids and into battle. . . "

"What are you saying, Darum? That he's dead?"

"No. We all believe – including Cook - that Uwomo and his horse are alive. I hear tell that he. . . uh, how to say this? . . . He disappeared. His horse too. A search party led by that Count could find no trace of the pair of them."

Manona feeling faint at hearing this, sways and topples over to collapse on the ground near to Macushla who cradles Manona's head on her lap and asks Darum to bring a cup of water to her.

Closing her eyes, Manona's sighs.

I knew it! His presence at the graves. . . it is a message from him. . . oh! praise be to the stars in heaven and may he live long and well.

Community

Yunitra's memories of fleeing, of being fearful and lonely have receded to a place at the back of her mind - except for the time she had spent working for the three midwives in the Lodge. Gratitude for their teachings and the trust they placed in her often returns: fleeting images of the great hearth in the Lodge, a cauldron of soup cooking over the fire bring a sense of comfort to her rather than regret. The way Elder Wise Woman tilts her head to listen to Yunitra's questions conjures a memory of Molly – the most forthright of the three midwives and whose wisdom sustained everybody in times of crisis. And still, at other times, these during the quiet of night while suckling Exacta, a tableau as finely wrought as a tapestry, fills her with inexplicable wonder: a sunlit glade on the edge of a dark forest where a soldier lay on Autumn leaves not far from his magnificent smoke-grey war horse grazing near the stream.

Little did I know at the time – being a fugitive fearful of detection and punishment that a gift was presented to me in that glade. Uwomo. Ah, and Maximus. Our dear Maximus. And then, there he was, standing on the crest of that headland in the dawn mist, ready to lead me through parts unknown to Uwomo. Oh Uwomo. . . my beloved mate and father of our children. . . Without knowing it, my own spirit lay open and receptive to being shown the way. . . I sense this receptivity to be trust. And here on this island, trust abounds.

Elder Wise Woman, recognizing the innate healer in Yunitra, had reached out to her, drawn her close, encouraged her to learn about the island's various healing plants. A keen learner, Yunitra has become confident under Elder Wise Woman's methodical instruction, adept at collecting medicinal plants, preparing these and ministering to the islanders.

Exacta, now seven years old, shows a natural ability towards tending to the ill and injured humans and, as it turns out, to all sentient beings. Although he is included in most games and adventures the island children engage in, he is most often found humming a tune while searching for plants, his small cotton sling bag over his shoulder. Exacta's lean, tawny-skinned body and wild curly hair resemble his mother's as does his penetrating blue-eyed gaze that seems to see deeply into Mother Nature's intricate, flawless design. Exacta is a quiet contemplative boy unless he is plying Yunitra with questions, such as: "Mama where do the flowers go when the fruit comes?" And "does Sister Moon know she is making the ocean come higher to shore?" Beneath his contemplative demeanor, bubbling like a mountain spring, is a most musical laugh that, once it erupts, seems to run away from him to become a torrent of uncontrollable joy, his eyes shining in merriment.

Uwomo is a solemn man. A deep, respectful thinker and staunch friend to the island men. He is also a steady, loving presence as a father and husband. Of his two children, it is Veritas, now ten years old, who cleaves to her father.

Working with the islanders on rebuilding the structures destroyed by that wall of ocean water he not only learned from Old Man Thunder about the nature and character of forest trees, he learned to select specific trees for building without disturbing the forest. He also became a skilled carpenter. The men had taken note of his ability and the pleasure he took in his work and had encouraged him to build a home for his family. The island men and women had assisted with the erection of a spacious one room home for his family with an added feature that Uwomo insisted upon: an enclosure attached to the side of the house for Maximus.

Throughout these days of working alongside others in a spirit of camaraderie Uwomo finds his thoughts harking back to the years he worked with Grandfather, to how much he discovered about himself and the art of blacksmithing. Seldom does he dwell on how that satisfying time had ended or how he had forced himself to befriend nobody in the barracks while disciplining his mind and body to become a revered warrior.

Most mornings at sunrise, Uwomo, Yunitra, Exacta, Veritas and Maximus meet on the beach to speak of themselves and the beauty of the world they are part of. On this particular morning Uwomo, startled awake by a dream in the predawn hours has gone ahead of his family and now sits on the rock where they like to meet.

The familiar sound of his children's voices bantering and laughing enters his contemplation as they run full tilt down the slope to him.

He listens for Yunitra's voice and for the steady hoof beats of Maximus that will surely follow.

Instead of her call that he likens to that of a turtle dove, he hears a cry of urgency in her tone.

"My beloved – look! There on the horizon."

Uwomo thinks, at first, that she has noticed the fishers in canoes beyond the breakwater, but on closer inspection he sees the billowing sails of an approaching ship.

The children join him and Yunitra on the rock. Maximus, his ears pricked, sniffs the air.

"Uwomo it's coming this way. I have an uncomfortable feeling about that vessel . . . Let's ask the children to go to the Elders to tell them."

"Hmmm. . . I don't like it either. Veritas, Exacta, you both know the homes of The Elders – yes?" They nod. "Please go to them as fast as you can and tell them about that sailing ship. Here, ride Maximus – he listens to you, Veritas. Off you go – ride like the wind and return here when you've given the Elders the message."

Uwomo and Yunitra stand close together as the fishing canoes frantically paddle away from the path of the ship that is now pitching and rolling in the waves at the breakwater.

The stiff breeze of early morning drops. The ship's sails collapse. Carried by waves, the ship continues to close the distance between the beach and the breakwater. Yunitra and Uwomo can now see figures running back and forth on the deck, they hear the sound of a released anchor chain followed by a splash. Islanders beach and secure their canoes and join Uwomo and Yunitra. In rapt silence they observe a rowboat lowered over the side of the ship, two oarsmen descend a rope ladder, settle into the boat and row to shore. The group on the beach grows in number as Old Man Thunder, Elder Wise Woman and fellow Elders join them. Maximus, the children on his back, stands as attentively as every human on that beach.

Both oarsmen negotiate a safe way between the shore rocks, jump into the shallows and heave the rowboat onto firm damp sand. Uwomo's scar on his cheek begins to throb. Yunitra's scalp tingles. Maximus turns his head in Uwomo's direction, snorts and paws at the ground.

Old Man Thunder steps out in front of his people gathered on the beach, raises his medicine staff to greet the two sailors that have come to a stop a few paces away, their hands raised open-palmed to declare they are unarmed and come in peace. Old Man Thunder, feathers on his medicine staff fluttering, offers a lengthy greeting to the sailors in the language of the island. When the older of the two sailors responds in the language of the world Uwomo and Yunitra had once inhabited, Uwomo moves to stand next to Old Man Thunder.

The sailor tells the group that they have an ill man on board who needs attention. This ill man will pay handsomely for medicine and treatment of his ailment as he is rich and an important man. The sailors request that the person most qualified on the island return immediately to the ship with them to minister to this ill man.

Uwomo translates for the islanders the sailor's explanation and request. Elder Wise Woman takes Yunitra by the hand, leads her to stand with her next to Old Man Thunder and asks Uwomo to make these inquiries: "Ask those two, please Uwomo, if others on the ship are ailing or if it is only this important man who is ill." Elder Wise Woman fears the possibility of contagion in the closed quarters of the ship which, if she and Yunitra were to board, could infect them and so spread to others in the island community.

It turns out that this important man fell ill soon after they set sail which, according to the sailor's account, would have been several months ago. The crew, aside from suffering extreme hunger, are not ill; only becoming weaker from lack of food and a depleted supply of drinking water.

Elder Wise Woman, now depending on Uwomo to translate, asks how the man's ailments affect him.

The older of the two sailors purses his mouth in disgust and proceeds to count off the ailments on his stubby fingers: "This man's bowels will not hold, he vomits blood, has a fever, and is wasting away. Sometimes he awakes screaming and raving. The two men who boarded the ship with this man, never leave his side except to call for wine or rum to calm him."

Uwomo remains implacable and translates. Elder Wise Woman faces the sailors, the strength of her wide body drawn to its full height, her arms extended towards them, states in a tone of voice that brooks no objection from anyone whatsoever:

"We will treat this man's ailments here on the island. We will not board the ship. Tell them, Uwomo, to bring the ill man here to this beach."

She turns to Old Man Thunder. "Fellow Elder, you will see to the building of a shelter over there", indicating a place in the shade of a small grove of trees, "And, you Veritas, will go with Exacta and the older children into the orchard and gardens. There you will collect three feast baskets of fruit and roots. These you will bring here. We will give the food to the sailors when they return with this ailing man."

Uwomo translates her statement to the sailors, but excludes, from his translation, her directions to the children. He is not certain as to why he does that – exclude the mention of food – but hopes it is not some previously undiscovered mean-spirited aspect of himself that is surfacing. He turns to Yunitra for her assessment of the situation.

Their eyes meet and he sees in her direct gaze, a veil of alarm but, welling up behind that, is her love for him and strength borne in kindness. She nods to him to indicate that she understands his exclusion as a precaution against a possible invasion by a starving crew. *Of course! Her assessment of this situation is intuitively keen and naturally protective. I saw that look in her eyes that night in the tower of stones when I confessed I was a deserter. Oh, my beloved, my cherished one. . .*

To be certain that the sailors would return to the ship immediately, three island men walk the sailors to the rowboat and assist their re-entry into the ocean.

The crowd not directly involved in the organization of building a shelter, disperse.

Exacta, Veritas and some older children set out for the orchard and gardens. Yunitra and Elder Wise Woman leave the beach to collect medicinal plants, salves, wash bowls and linens from the healing house to bring to the shelter that is already in the process of being erected. Old Man Thunder, accompanied by fellow Elders and Uwomo, remain on the beach to wait for the children to return with baskets of food and to be ready for the return of the rowboat that will bear the 'important' man. The island men, perplexed and also curious, gaze at the sky as if an explanation could be there, then at the ocean as if that is where some comprehension could be found. Uwomo is uneasy.

Old Man Thunder is aware of Uwomo's uneasiness indicated by the way his right fist repeatedly massages that scar. Old Man Thunder has not seen this form of contemplative concern in the man for some years; this tall, strong, solemn and truthful man he would trust with his life. He beckons to Uwomo to join him a few paces away from the others. "Uwomo, tell me how it is that you know the language of the sailors and what it is that worries you about that sailing ship in our waters."

"Ah, my venerable friend, the language the sailors speak is the tongue of the land of my birth and also that of Yunitra. Memories of my life there have dimmed but, the appearance of those sailors and the ship anchored out there. . . uh, how do I say this? It is as if a flame within me is igniting . . . umm, a flame akin to the call of combat. This I do not wish to engage in – combat, that is – and without my sword – it was taken by Mother Ocean – I am as vulnerable as Turtle lying on her back".

"You are only as vulnerable as your fear is of being that, Uwomo. And, in any case, whoever this 'important' man is, he is ill and infirm. Stay close to me and together we will observe and act accordingly. Did you inform the sailors of our offer of food?"

"No, I did not. I was uncertain of my reasoning until Yunitra, in her intuitive way, supported my excluding that from translation. Only then did I realize that I am fearful that the entire ship's crew might come ashore, driven by hunger and thirst and, possibly, there are other reasons unclear to me."

"I see now that you do not trust these people whose language you speak." Uwomo lowered his eyes, raked his fingers through his thick greying curls, sighed and, returning his gaze to Old Man Thunder's piercing look, he nodded an assent.

"I also do not trust them, Uwomo. Be certain of that. So, we will all need to be vigilant while practicing courtesy. . . and, oho! look, the rowboat is returning. That took little time – huh? – a favourable tide, maybe? Be still in your heart, Uwomo. Together we will all take care of this unexpected visitation. We will ask the children – whenever they come with the food – hmmm. . . I wonder where they are - to place the food behind the shelter – not down here on the beach. And now it is time to call Yunitra, Elder Wise Woman and others to assist us."

Islanders spring into action: fishers assist the sailors to beach their rowboat, Yunitra and Elder Wise Woman arrive, the children stow the baskets of food behind the shelter now ready to receive its patient, Uwomo follows Old Man Thunder to meet the ill man.

The sailors lift a canvas stretcher from the rowboat on which lies a prone body under a light sheet, a damp cloth covering the patient's face.

"Carry him directly to that shelter you see over there." commands Elder Wise Woman. Yunitra translates. The sailors walk fast to the shelter. Yunitra breaks into a run to reach the shelter before them. Elder Wise Woman follows with Uwomo and Old Man Thunder. As the sailors reach the entrance of the shelter a gust of wind blows the cloth off the face of the man on the stretcher. Uwomo stops dead in his stride, recognition churns his guts.

Count Arrogar's eyelids flutter and open. His dull bloodshot eyes, dart from side to side then alight on Uwomo who turns away from the Count and vomits on the ground. The Count is seized by a paroxysm that stiffens his limbs, causes his head to thrash about, white foam coats his lips. Elder Wise Woman gestures to the sailors to place the stretcher in the shelter and to move out of her way.

"Quick, Yunitra, a swab soaked in the brain fever tea. Straddle him, hold his hands down flat on either side of his head while I squeeze drops from the tea-soaked swab into his mouth."

Uwomo turns back to face his nemesis only to see his beloved astride the Count's body struggling to maintain a hold on the Count's hands. He strides over to Yunitra and whispers: "My beloved, I will do this. Step away from him now."

Uwomo grips the Count's hands, pins them on either side of the Count's head, and straddles him. The weight of Uwomo's body bears down on the Count's thighs and hips. Elder Wise Woman ministers the tea between the Count's lips that he hungrily licks at and then swallows until he is calm and lies still.

Old Man Thunder beckons to the sailors and to Uwomo to follow him to a tree far from the shelter. Here, the four men sit facing each other.

"Uwomo, you may wish to not answer the question I will now put to you in the presence of these two sailors. If not, you and I can speak of it later. This is my question: this ailing man – this man whom we are told is an important man – recognizes you. Who is he?"

"With respect, venerable friend, I would prefer to hear the sailors' account of this man's presence on their ship and the reason for the voyage they have embarked upon, before I respond to your question."

Old Man Thunder nods in agreement and indicates to Uwomo that he put his queries to the sailors.

The sailors' account, begins hesitantly, soon spills out in a torrent of words from both sailors. While Uwomo listens, having decided to not interrupt the sailors with translation until they finish, Old Man Thunder scrutinizes the men, his head cocked to the side listening to the tone of their voices.

According to the sailors, Count Arrogar had fallen ill while still in command of the barracks. The church authorities ordered the Count to travel to the coast to recuperate. On arrival at the coast, the Count paid a vast amount of money to the captain for passage for himself and his body-guards aboard that ship now anchored in island waters. The purpose of the voyage, instigated by authorities of the church was to convert savages – that is how the church describes people in other lands - to believing in their god.

At this juncture in their account Uwomo takes advantage of the moment to translate to Old Man Thunder whose response is unexpected. "This kind of ship is not new to me. It was people of that ilk, on a ship like this one, who brought devastation, disease and greed to where we Elders lived when we were young. We do not forget our escape nor those whom we lost. We are wise not to trust them. Tell these sailors that they can leave us now. We will provide them with the food the children gathered. They will leave the Count here under our care. As soon as he improves – or not – we will raise a blue flag to signal that they return for him. Tell them that, please Uwomo, and send them away. When they are gone, you and I will then speak about the demons this man, this Count, arouses in you."

Once they were certain that the sailors were well on their way back to the ship,

Uwomo reveals, to Old Man Thunder, the role Count Arrogar had played in his young life. While recounting that day that he deserted, Uwomo's face colors with a rush of shame that Old Man Thunder notices, his heart filling with empathy. Uwomo stumbles in his telling and then stops speaking.

"O-hu-zhuto! Uwomo! I see that moment in your life as if it had happened to me. When a man is face to face with an enemy. . . an enemy that causes him to fear becoming an enemy to himself, in truth, he is being offered a gift. The gift is a path of hope and courage. This you did by deserting the demons of death in order to find the light of life."

As the word "life" springs from his mouth, Old Man Thunder's body tips backwards to lie spread-eagled, he raises his legs in the air, his feet dance a jig as if the sky were his floor and he breaks into an uproarious laugh: so deep and loud is his laugh, Uwomo is convinced the gods of thunder have just cracked a joke.

Aha! This old man is in deed appropriately named.

And from the heat of his shame that had risen from the pit of his gut, Uwomo now experiences laughter rising – laughter that obliterates self recrimination: a laugh that pours from him like an unblocked river flowing in full spate.

Maximus, Veritas and Exacta come upon the two men lying on their backs, splayed like a pair of sea stars, laughing uproariously. Benevolent smiles on both men's faces clearly indicate that nothing untoward is occurring. Old Man Thunder and Uwomo , on hearing that the evening meal is ready, accompany Maximus, Veritas and Exacta to the communal eating hall.

Release.

Although wary of that ship anchored just beyond the breakwater, islanders are also relieved to have had no visitors from the ship for several days. The sailors must have conveyed Old Man Thunder's order to the captain that no person was to visit until a blue flag was raised.

Meanwhile Count Arrogar's health is steadily declining. It is clear to both Yunitra and Elder Wise Woman that although he no longer vomits blood, his body is ruined beyond repair. During brief bouts of lucidity, the Count babbles about a sword, a shield in a fire, the loss of his prize warrior and most often weeps over being mocked by soldiers. As Elder Wise Woman does not know his language, she listens to the tone of his confused iterations and waits for Yunitra to explain.

One afternoon while Yunitra is resting next to Uwomo before returning to the shelter to relieve Elder Wise woman, she recalls the time when she and Uwomo and Maximus were observing the Count from the cleft in the tower of rocks. She mentions one incident in particular that now comes to mind: The Count, apparently calm, is seated on a cushion on a log, his feet to the fire, contemplating something resting on his lap. A soldier returns from the flat-topped rock on the crest of the hill, approaches the Count and in response to something the Count says – a question, perhaps – the soldier shakes his head. The Count flies into a rage and flings the object from his lap into the fire. The soldier hangs his head and stares into the flames.

"Beloved," she says to Uwomo, "the shield in a fire that the Count weeps and rages about - could that have been your shield that you had hurled into a river when you were discarding all your battle armor? Maybe it was discovered by the Count and his search party. He would have recognized it - don't you think? Pity that we couldn't see, from where we were hiding, what it was that he threw into the fire."

"That surely could have been my shield he was holding in his lap. But why would he then willfully destroy it? In all these episodes of raving you describe to me, a pattern is forming of a man losing his mind in the pits of hell."

"That may be so, Uwomo which is why I feel the time has come for you to visit the Count. For all I know, it could be you, dearly beloved, who is this "prize warrior" he mourns the loss of. And what's more. . . do you recall the sailors speaking of the church authorities ordering the Count to leave the barracks? Could it be that the soldiers are no longer hunting and killing? Could it be that the raids have ceased?"

She's right about my visiting the Count − I know that it is something I must do and trust her judgement implicitly but . . . why am I so strongly against being seen by him? There is nothing he can do about my desertion now and if, as Yunitra says, the raids have ceased, the barracks have fallen into disuse . . . could that mean that actions to have me punished can no longer be carried out? I am thankful for the absence from our island of his bodyguards for they surely would find a way to destroy me. May they remain on the ship and out of my sight!

Count Arrogar's body aches from fighting the demons devouring him, mocking him in cruel sniggers. As he surfaces from that dark horror and returns to his surroundings, he becomes aware of light filtering through the smoke hole in the shelter roof. A soft sheet covering his prone body carries a familiar fragrance of crushed cedar and lemon grass indicating that he has recently been bathed by the two women who tend to him night and day. Although comfortable to a certain degree, he is still in the grip of a nauseating fear. He wants to die. He wonders why he continues to live. He wishes to be released from the torment of inner conflict over which he has exerted his control for most of his life.

The figure of a man fills the shelter doorway then enters and approaches the Count lying on his cot. A second figure, his arm raised to grasp a staff topped with feathers, hovers in the doorway. The Count turns his head to the man now kneeling at his side. As recognition dawns, the Count's sneer, well remembered by Uwomo, melts into a grin that shows rotten teeth below his untended ragged blonde moustache. Uwomo is shocked by the man's physical decline: corded neck, thin arms and boney shoulders that give him the appearance of a ghoul; a ghoul with a glint of cunning in the eyes.

"Uwomo?"

"It is I, Uwomo, Count Arrogar."

"How can this be? Reassure me that you are not an apparition. . . that you are a living full-bodied man."

"Here, take my hand, Count Arrogar."

The Count grabs a hold of Uwomo's hand at which Uwomo stifles a surge of disgust with his nemesis who is now clutching at Uwomo's fingers. "Indeed you are not an apparition! Oh, Uwomo, how I have missed you. . ." The Count breaks into convulsive sobbing.

Uwomo withdraws his hand from the Count's weakening grip and rises to stand over the Count.

"I also wish to be reassured, Count Arrogar - reassured of your clemency in the face of my desertion from your army. As you seem to be close to the end of your life I wish to be granted clemency before you die. That is all I have to say to you."

The Count wipes his face and runny nose on a corner of the sheet covering him. In a hoarse whisper, shades of his coercive ways showing, he begs: "Uwomo, I will grant you clemency in return for your forgiveness. Will you do that for me – forgive me?"

"I am able to do that, Count Arrogar only because I have found the courage to forgive myself for following your orders for as long as I did."

"You are? You forgive me?" The Count closes his eyes. "Thank you, Uwomo. Now I can die in a modicum of peace – although that sublime state of being is unknown to me if truth be told."

Uwomo makes ready to leave the shelter but the Count's arm snakes towards him with unexpected agility, grabs a hold of Uwomo's wrist. "But don't leave me so soon Uwomo stay with me a while longer . . . stay with me until I depart this world, would you?"

Was this challenge to my compassion written in the stars? Am I fit for the task of easing this man's passage into the next world? What would Manona advise me to do? I suspect she would tell me that I have no alternative but to be present for this man's passing.

As if in reply to these questions, a fleeting image of himself preparing to die in the deep darkness of Mother Ocean, whips through his mind. He acknowledges the Count's request and agrees to remain with him.

Throughout the day Yunitra brings water for Uwomo and a calming brew for her patient who has not spoken since receiving Uwomo's forgiveness.

In the lingering shadows of a day folding into night, Uwomo's vigil comes to a close as Count Arrogar surrenders to death.

Yunitra and Elder Wise Woman bathe the Count before wrapping him in a shroud. Old Man Thunder raises the blue flag. Uwomo stands on the beach, Maximus close by, waiting for his children and beloved wife to join him. Soon the sailors will arrive to take Count Arrogar's body for burial at sea.

O-hu-Zhuto!

CPSIA information can be obtained
at www.ICGtesting.com
Printed in the USA
BVHW031218060620
580988BV00001B/42

9 781525 566448